A KILLING NIGHT

The fog pressed in on them, cold and secretive. They were alone on the moor, alone in the world. And suddenly Bill was aware that the footsteps of his companion no longer sounded beside his own.

"Where the devil have you got to?" he said, and heard a car start up at some little distance. As the engine roared and the headlights swung toward him, he knew panic. Even as he turned away, blindly, frantically, the car increased its speed. He did not see the blurred lights that followed him, nor the shape of the car looming at last out of the mist. But he felt the force of the impact and an eternity of pain . . .

ERROR OF THE MOON

Sara Woods

AVON
PUBLISHERS OF BARD, CAMELOT, DISCUS AND FLARE BOOKS

AVON BOOKS
A division of
The Hearst Corporation
1790 Broadway
New York, New York 10019

Copyright © 1963 by Sara Woods
Published by arrangement with the author
Library of Congress Catalog Card Number: 85-91540
ISBN: 0-380-69859-5

First Avon Printing, June 1986

AVON TRADEMARK REG. U. S. PAT. OFF. AND IN OTHER COUNTRIES, MARCA
REGISTRADA, HECHO EN U.S.A.

Printed in the U.S.A.

K–R   10   9   8   7   6   5   4   3   2   1

"It is the very error of the moon;
   She comes more near the earth than she was wont,
   And makes men mad."

OTHELLO, Act V, Scene II.

AUTHOR'S NOTE

In the last days of Queen Victoria's reign, a good deal of doubt existed as to whether permission would be given for the railway to lay a track up Washburndale, or whether the area would be taken over to provide an additional water supply for the city of Leeds. In the event, the Waterworks carried the day, and the three "reservoys"—Linley, Farnley and Fewston—are there to demonstrate the victory.

But this story is set in the upper reaches of the dale, where there are few people now to be offended by the liberties I have taken. It is not, perhaps, too imaginative to think that a town something like Mardingley might have grown out of the cluster of lace-makers' cottages and the now-ruined mill . . . if the railway had won instead, and a line now ran through Norwood Bottom, past Hanging Slade, and West End, and Thruscross, over to Ap'tr'ick Moor.

S.W.

CHAPTER ONE

THE CARCROFT WORKS of General Aircraft Limited stand on the moor above Mardingley, about five miles along the road which leaves the town by Felgate. On a clear night the glare of the floodlights forms a pool in the surrounding darkness, but on this November afternoon the fog had come creeping: across the moor, through the high wire fence; with prying, inquisitive fingers that sought out every corner of the sheds and muffled sight and sound so that the plant stood isolated.

By nightfall the Transport Division had closed its doors, and the drivers had departed, for the most part on foot, towards the town. Only Sir Thomas's chauffeur remained and cursed his employer's contrariness to the commissionaire on duty in the front hall. Nightshift was being worked in No. 3 shed, and the sound of the machines came to them faintly. "Wonder they got 'ere, any on 'em," said Ambler, the commissionaire, who was a local man.

Young Bill Homer left the Research laboratory at a little after eight-thirty. He began to cough as the fog met him, and was still coughing when he passed the gatehouse. "Nasty night, sir," said the sergeant. "It is, an' all," said Bill, absently.

He should, of course, have taken the lift Stephen offered; his excuse was genuine enough, he *had* wanted to see the finish of that series of runs. But there had been the thought, too, "supposing he asks me——" So now there was nothing for it but to walk, with his bewildered, uneasy thoughts for company. He buttoned up the collar of his raincoat and paused a moment, trying to accustom his eyes to the darkness beyond the circle of fog-dimmed lights.

1

"It's no night for walking," said a voice beside him.

Bill turned with something like a jump. "What . . . oh, I thought you'd gone long since."

"Nervy, old boy? I've been talking to Harry, and lucky for you. Come along."

"It's not much of a night for driving, either." Bill's tone made a fair attempt at lightness as he fell into step beside his companion and turned towards the car park. The other man said airily:

"There's gratitude for you! I'm right over the other side somewhere."

The fog pressed in on them, cold and secretive. The lights were obscured long ago, they were alone on the moor, alone in the world. And suddenly Bill was aware that the footsteps of his companion no longer sounded beside his own. He stopped, and said "Here!" on a note of protest, and peered round anxiously into the mist.

The other man laughed. "Over here, old boy. Not that way, you fool," he added impatiently. "Can't you see me?"

"I can't see anything!" said Bill; and was again shaken by a fit of coughing. He added hoarsely, when he could speak again: "Where the devil have you got to?" and heard, as he spoke, a car start up at some little distance. He thought, irritably, who else has been fool enough to stay as late as this?

"Stay where you are." His companion's voice was farther away now. Already the fog was blanketing the distance between them, stretching the few yards to an immeasurable expanse. "I've got a torch somewhere, *I*'ll find you."

The car was moving now, but cautiously, its engine idling. Queer how difficult it was to estimate distance; it seemed to have gone past them towards the entrance, but now it was near again, and Bill saw, faintly, the glow of the headlights, blurred and softened in the mist. His companion said: "There!" loudly (but had he really come any nearer?), and a gentle beam of light came stabbing through the fog in his direction, wavered, and settled steadily to illumine the hem of his raincoat. Bill was conscious of relief, out of all proportion to the seriousness of his position. If the night was his enemy (and his state of mind, though he did not know it, was a long way from normal), this gleam was, most surely, his friend. He had only to wait. . . .

But the other man was silent now, though the flashlight glowed steadily. The car was still circling cautiously, and then suddenly there was a change. The engine note speeded, tyres hissed on the damp tarmac as the steering-wheel was wrenched round. Bill, turning towards the sound, saw the lights approaching, and moved a little out of the line of the car's advance. Though he did not know it, the beam of the hand-torch followed him, dim but inexorably revealing.

As the engine roared and the headlights swung towards him again he knew panic. They looked monstrous now, malignant. The man who had offered to drive him was forgotten; here was only a machine for enemy, he had no thought for the man who drove it. And now the darkness, which he had feared a moment since, should have stood his friend; but even as he turned away, blindly, frantically, the car increased its speed. He was running now, in a futile effort to escape. He did not see the blurred lights that followed him, nor the shape of the car looming at last out of the mist. But he heard the roar of the engine, and he felt the force of the impact and an eternity of pain; before the darkness closed about him, and the moor was silent again.

CHAPTER TWO

ANTONY MAITLAND, falling for a moment beyond the orbit of the conversation, regarded his visitors with a degree of amusement only slightly tempered by the analogy which had occurred to him between the depleted condition of the decanter and the equally depressed state of his current account; short of an unexpected "refresher" (and his clerk had admittedly sound ideas on the subject of fees), no replenishment of either would be forthcoming for at least a fortnight.

Once he had heard from George the invitation had been, of course, inevitable. One does not lightly turn an old acquaintance from one's doors; and when he has travelled some two hundred miles for the express purpose of asking advice, the least that can be done is to wine him and dine him to the best of one's ability.

Considered purely as a reunion, the evening could not be said to be an unqualified success. George Ramsey seemed to have acquired an air of consequence which Antony (remembering their schooldays) felt he should have expected. The war years and his subsequent business career notwithstanding, he had been, and remained, a bore. His companion, Stephen Naylor, was a sardonic-looking fellow who seemed to have no great facility in casual conversation. Altogether, Antony felt, it was a shame to have inflicted them on his wife; though Jenny, rising to the occasion, was doing her share, and more than her share of the necessary work. Regarding her with affection, he might himself suspect that her look of breathless interest masked only a complete blankness of mind; or, at best, that she was considering a new seasoning for braised

4

kidneys, or whether it would be best to have the Jaguar's engine decarbonised now, or in the spring. But certainly George, sunning himself complacently in the warmth of her attention, could have no such suspicion.

The anecdote came to an end. Jenny said "What a shame!" in tones so heartfelt that Antony wondered for a moment whether she was not over-playing her part a little. Stephen Naylor moved suddenly, impatiently, shifting his position in the shabby wing chair and clearing his throat. George glanced at him, and then back at his hostess. "Yes . . . well!" he said.

"It's time we got down to business," said Stephen, without apology. "George told you, Maitland, we need your help." He looked in his turn at Jenny, and added only slightly less abruptly, "It's important, or I wouldn't have inflicted myself on you like this."

Jenny, seeing no reply to this that would not be quite devastating in its triteness, contented herself with smiling at him; and after a moment Stephen relaxed a little and grinned back at her. His voice was much less testy when he spoke again to his companion. "Come on, George, out with it. It was your idea, after all."

George seemed to be suffering a quite unaccountable diffidence. Antony decided it was time to sacrifice the remainder of the brandy, in the interest of getting the problem (whatever it might be) at least propounded some time before midnight. Stephen met his questioning look with a slight shake of the head; George's glass was filled and Antony said as he went to resume his seat:

"Some legal problem, I take it."

"Not exactly," said George.

"You said," Antony pointed out, "that you wanted my advice." Something in Ramsey's voice had alerted him; he no longer sounded easy-going, and the look he turned on Stephen Naylor was bright and questioning. "And *you* said 'my help'," he added. "Which do you mean?"

"Well . . . both." It was George who replied, and he spoke with the ponderous air of one whose words have been well-weighed. Stephen, looking from one to the other of them with more interest than he had hitherto displayed, thought he would have put ten years between their ages, at a guess, had he not known them to be contemporaries. Ramsey had matured into the almost perfect type of younger executive; a solid citizen, older than his years. For all that, he was a good enough chap, and Stephen felt for him the rather contemptuous liking that was the nearest he had allowed himself to approach to friendship for some years now. Maitland, though: that was a different matter altogether. He must be thirty-six—thirty-seven?—though he looked younger; a tall, dark fellow with a thin, intelligent face and a pleasantly casual manner. But there had been nothing casual in the way he had taken them up just now; and though his expression of polite interest faded to one of blankness as George spoke, so that nothing remained to tell what he was thinking, still there was left an impression of wariness, of a caution that was unexpected. Stephen, accustomed to judging his fellow men summarily, and dismissing them for the most part as only too easily read, was aware of the first stirrings of curiosity.

"You see," George was saying, "it isn't as a lawyer we want to consult you. It's because—this is going back a good way, but after all—you were on intelligence work in the army, weren't you?"

Antony got up. It was a sudden movement, and he realised with surprise that an instinct of flight had brought him to his feet: a feeling as absurd as it was untenable. George could have nothing to say that could in any way touch him; hear what it was all about then; advise if he could, and if he cared to; and forget it again. He settled a shoulder against the mantelpiece, and said "Yes" in a tone that was only mildly repressive.

George looked up at him, and spread his hands in a peculiarly helpless gesture. "We've got a problem," he said. "A leak," he amplified.

"My dear Ramsey, I'm not a plumber!"

"A leakage of information. You know perfectly well what I mean." George was indignant, but retained his grasp of essentials. The retort, however, had so far carried him back to his schooldays that his reply came in much the same strain. "It's jolly important, young Maitland, so don't look down your nose at me," he said firmly. Antony grinned at him.

"I'm sorry," he apologised. "But all this circumlocution, it really was irresistible. Suppose you try coming to the point."

Stephen Naylor had been following this exchange, not troubling to hide his amusement. He turned to look at his hostess, in whom he had observed already a sharp sense of the ridiculous. There was now, however, no gleam of appreciation in her eye; her hands were clasped tightly in her lap, and she was looking at her husband with unmistakable anxiety. She was quite unconscious that she, in turn, was being studied, and Stephen allowed himself to look at her for longer than would normally be considered good manners. When he had met Jenny Maitland that evening, his first thought had been: Good lord, she's a beauty! and though he had since revised this opinion a little he still felt that she was one of the nicest girls he had ever seen. Jenny had brown curls and a slender figure; candid grey eyes, and an air of serenity that only now seemed to have deserted her. She turned and met his scrutiny, and just for a moment she looked lost; but then she met his regard steadily.

"You'll tell us, Mr. Naylor," she suggested.

Stephen thought her voice as calm as ever, but looking up again at Antony Maitland he saw the amusement fade from the other man's expression, and a frown replace it.

"What about it, Naylor?" he asked, quietly. "Ramsey seems strangely incoherent, and I'm becoming curious."

"It's quite simple, really," said Stephen. He paused, and favoured his audience, for the first time that evening, with a smile that was free of cynicism, and singularly attractive. "Though you might not think it," he added.

Antony moved a little, away from the heat of the fire. "Tell us," he invited. He glanced again, briefly, at Jenny; his eyes, as they returned to Stephen's face, were expressionless, but his manner had hardened. He was tense, not casual any longer. And when he added, "We're all agog!" the younger man thought he recognised, behind the light tone, a bitter echo of his own manner.

"You know the firm we're with—General Aircraft," he began. "We're up at Mardingley, in Yorkshire, about half an hour's drive from Harrogate——"

"If you don't get involved with the confounded local bus service," said George, with feeling.

"Yes, well, I don't know if you're familiar with that part——"

"I know it quite well." Antony looked from one to the other of his visitors, and his look of amusement returned, deepening the lines about his mouth, as he realised ruefully that unless he took a hand in the matter the story seemed likely to remain untold. And how little he wished to hear it. "Perhaps I can help you," he offered. "Mardingley is a small town on the moors, and General Aircraft established themselves there in the early days of the war. And there they remain; I take it they've grown?"

"Nearly six thousand employees!" George's tone was an invitation to find the figure impressive.

"I also suppose—in view of your somewhat incoherent remarks a moment ago—that they are now engaged in some operation on the secret list. What's your job, Ramsey?"

"Assistant Works Manager," said George, and cleared his throat.

"You should add that your particular sphere of influence is the Missile Division," Stephen put in.

"Thank you. Now your job, Naylor, may be one which requires clarity of thought; but it does not seem to be one which encourages clarity of expression." His tone was inquiring, and Stephen laughed.

"I run the computer group, that's on the Research side," he said. "And you're quite right, self-expression isn't my strong suit."

"However, we progress. Now, this leak of yours——"

"I put it too strongly." George spoke with sudden decision. "We don't really know——"

"We know enough." Stephen's interruption was incisive and unceremonious. "The first thing was three months back, Maitland——"

"What happened?"

"We got instructions to check our procedure, to tighten up generally." It was George who answered, and he did so with a look at his colleague that conveyed exasperation. "That's nothing new. Then a chap came down from the Ministry, they really were serious about it; he said some information had come back to them from an unauthorised source, wanted to know whether we'd communicated it yet to the sub-contractors; that kind of thing."

"And had you?"

"No. As a matter of fact, the only people who really knew this particular fact were Stephen here, and a couple of his chaps. So——"

"That made it tricky, as you can imagine."

"I may start to exercise my imagination," said Antony tartly, "when you give me something to work on." He looked at George, who showed signs of being affronted, and then turned back to the younger of the visitors. "These chaps of yours, now——?"

"Tom Burns and Bill Homer. Both good lads, both safe as houses—I'd have said. Tom came to us four years ago, from Bristol—the university, I mean, not B.A.C. Bill was an ex-apprentice."

"Was there anything on paper?"

"There were drawings, of course."

"Which any of your colleagues could have understood?"

"Well, yes, I suppose so."

"And what was the result of the investigation?"

"Nothing at all." George sounded aggrieved. "They played merry hell with our targets for a fortnight, and then went away talking about 'coincidences'."

"They could have been right." He turned to look down at the fire, and stirred it with his foot so that the flames leaped and danced.

"So we thought. Well, you know how it is: you never think anything can go wrong among people you know," said Stephen.

"I envy your lightheartedness. However, something made you change your minds?"

"Something else happened," George admitted. "A letter went missing; well, just for a day as a matter of fact——"

"That doesn't sound very impressive."

"It was because it came on top of the other." Stephen's reluctance seemed to have vanished, and he spoke freely enough. "The envelope was marked 'Secret'; that meant it came to us via the Secretary's office. I was with Weston when Mickey brought it over—that was about ten o'clock. I got back to the lab about eleven." He paused, and looked at George, and added with an air of defiance: "The letter wasn't on my desk then."

George seemed flustered. "Now, Stephen, old boy, I only said——"

"Well, I know I didn't look for it." Stephen's tone was elaborately reasonable, but from the glitter in his eye Antony judged the point to have been a contentious one. "Why should I?"

"You weren't expecting anything?"

"No. At least I knew Rymer's would be sending us their spec. some time. But I didn't know when."

"But the thing is——" George retained his air of apology, but his voice was firmer now, as though he had reached a decision. "The thing is, they were a week past their deadline. And you *had* been cheating about it."

"So you have reminded me, only too often!" If Ramsey had made up his mind to a policy of plain speaking, clearly his younger colleague had no intention of allowing his remarks to pass unchallenged. "If you think——"

"I merely want to make clear to Maitland the position as it appeared to the security chaps," George retorted. "If *I* thought anything of it I shouldn't have brought you here."

"Well, I'm sorry." Neither Stephen's voice nor his countenance was really expressive of contrition. "But I would have noticed the envelope, you know. It was one of those big, brown ones."

"So, sometime between—say—ten o'clock and eleven, it disappeared. You mentioned 'specifications,' didn't you? Were they important?"

"Apparently," said George, and looked at Stephen as though for confirmation. Stephen said, unwillingly:

"Not in themselves. Only in conjunction with what we knew; Bill, and Tom, and myself." He looked at George, and added bitterly: "That was another thing the security people found interesting."

"I'm sure it was. But you haven't told me—when did you discover the envelope was missing?"

"Rogers telephoned; he's the Deputy Chief Engineer at Rymer's and he wanted to know if we liked what they'd done, and of course I said the letter hadn't arrived——" He paused, and his expression was forbidding as he went on: "But after I'd rung off Carleton came across and said 'hadn't it been one of Rymer's envelopes Mickey brought over?'; and then Evan chipped in, and we started to look for it."

"Things do get mislaid."

"Of course they do." He sounded impatient. "Only after what had happened . . . well, we finished up by practically taking the place apart. It just wasn't there!"

"It still seems rather drastic to assume——"

"What would you have thought?" Stephen retorted. George said, pacifically:

"It was Akeroyd who insisted we call them in again."

"And what did 'they' say?"

"They arrived next morning," said Stephen. "A chap called Milner, to be exact, and a couple of satellites. The first thing that happened was that they found the missing envelope in the bottom left-hand drawer of my desk."

"Had it been opened?"

"Nothing to show. It can be done, I expect . . . I don't need to tell you."

"Contents?"

"All complete." He added, with the suspicion of a grin, "I don't think Milner was any too pleased."

"He didn't believe you?"

"No, he didn't. He thought we were crying 'wolf'."

"Well, it was reasonable enough, I suppose, from his point of view," said George. "He hadn't helped look for the damned thing."

"No, but we had. Damn it, Maitland, we all *knew* it wasn't there."

"Certainty's a very fine thing." Antony's tone was deprecating. "But I must admit at this point my sympathies are with Milner. What happened next?"

George Ramsey showed signs of taking offence, and started on a rather disjointed protest. But Naylor interrupted him, saying brusquely: "That's easily told. Bill Homer was killed!"

The words sounded oddly in the warm, shabby room. Antony's eyes were intent now; he noted Stephen's look of defiance, as though his statement was a challenge; George's expression was uneasy, he seemed to be doubting the wisdom of his colleague's bluntness; and Jenny's hands locked suddenly together, locked and tightened. Antony became aware of anger. He said, too quietly: "If you mean, he was murdered, you may as well say so."

Stephen looked up at him, conscious of the change of tone. "*I* think so. George doesn't. It *could* have been an accident," he admitted.

"He was knocked down by a car on a foggy night," said George. "It happens all the time."

"On our car park," said Stephen. "Someone knew what had happened!"

"But that doesn't mean——"

"On top of the other things?" Stephen sounded savage. He turned again to his host, and his tone made only the faintest concession towards conventional courtesy. "I can't *make* you believe me. But I'm quite certain——"

"I take it, then, no proof was forthcoming for either theory?"

"No," said Ramsey. "The inquest brought in 'Accident,' and that's what we all thought. Except Stephen."

"I don't like coincidences myself. Had you any other reason for your disbelief?"

Stephen took his time about replying, but said at length: "I could have believed in suicide, only not that way. And I couldn't believe in accident because what was he doing there, he hadn't a car? So it had to be murder." He was ignoring George now, and addressed himself to Antony;

but added, in irritation perhaps at his host's unresponsive look, "Bill was a good chap; but something was wrong, I don't know what."

Jenny's curls shone gold in the lamplight; her hands were very white against the dark green of her dress. George looked, incomprehensibly, both stubborn and alarmed. Stephen's voice had a sharpness, but he was only saying one half—perhaps?—of what was in his mind; his mouth had a bitter twist, but his eyes were anxious. Antony said, into the uneasy silence; "Even if we grant all you say and all you assume . . . why have you come to me?"

"Because we hoped . . . George said——"

"I thought," said George, on his dignity, "that at least you'd advise us."

"What can I say? If the experts can do nothing, it's up to you. Tighten on security, and wait on the event."

"That's not so easy." Stephen looked at George, and added with an air of desperation: "Any action we took . . . we'd have to trust each other!"

Surprisingly, Ramsey took this calmly, though with a deprecating look at Jenny. "Unfortunately, that's true enough," he said. "And things can't go on as they are; you must see that."

"I see your problem," said Antony. "But I don't see where I come in."

"We want you to come to Mardingley," said George, and sat back, suddenly at ease, to watch the effect of his words. Antony abandoned his lounging position, and with it any affectation of languor. He looked older now, Stephen thought, and both guarded and dangerous; and his tone was biting when he spoke.

"May I remind you, Ramsey, that my connection with Intelligence was a purely war-time one."

"That wasn't what the general told our Josiah," said George, with an air of triumph.

"The general?"

"Wright. The war wasn't so long ago that you've forgotten him?" he queried, blandly sarcastic.

"Of course not." Antony brushed the question aside. "What did he say?" he demanded. And now there was evident in his manner an uncertainty—more than that, an anxiety—which his anger a few moments ago had covered.

"He said that on one occasion at least they'd called you in as what he called a legal consultant in some affair or other."

"Yes," said Antony. He spoke quietly, but his eyes shifted away from his visitors; it seemed as if with the one word he gave up the initiative, so that the discussion was Ramsey's, to direct as he would.

"What happened once," said George pontifically, following his advantage, "can happen again."

Antony looked at Jenny then. "I'm sorry, love," he said as though they had been alone. And then, almost casually, over his shoulder, "I won't do it, you know."

"Now look here, Maitland——"

Stephen interrupted him. "You haven't heard what we're suggesting," he pointed out.

"And I don't want to." The words lacked polish, but he sounded merely tired.

Jenny looked up as he spoke. It was so long since she had withdrawn from the conversation that they were all a little surprised at her re-entry into it. "I think you should listen to them," she said. She met her husband's regard steadily, and after a moment her attitude lost its tension, and she leaned back again in her corner of the sofa.

Antony turned back to George. He still looked troubled, and his offer was far from enthusiastic. "All right then, I'll hear what you propose," he said. "But I make no promises."

Ramsey took his time about replying. "Josiah wants a thorough inquiry," he said. "He talked to Wright, and Wright mentioned you. So——"

"So he thought you might have a pull with me, and sent you to use it," Antony broke in. "You needn't trouble to wrap it up; in fact, I'd rather you didn't."

"So, naturally enough, he asked me to see you." George seemed to feel that the interruption would be best ignored. "The idea is that you would come to Mardingley——"

"In what capacity? I mean," he added, with exaggerated patience, as Ramsey looked blank, "do you propose I

should come down with full credentials from the Ministry
and a blaze of publicity; or are you suggesting a hole-and-
corner affair?''

"Well," said George.

"The latter, obviously." Antony answered his own question. "Well, I thought as much." There fell a brief,
uncomfortable silence. "Who is this Josiah of yours,
anyway?''

"Josiah Akeroyd," said Stephen.

"Chief Engineer," Ramsey explained. "A good chap,
though perhaps a trifle—well—eccentric.''

"I'm sorry," said Antony. "He sounds quite fascinating, but even so——"

"You won't even consider it? After all, you know, it is
important—the work we're doing.''

"If you wait a moment longer," said Stephen to his
host, "you'll hear old George pulling out all the patriotic
stops.''

"It's all very well for you to sneer," said Ramsey.
"You were keen enough on coming.''

"Of course I was! You seem to forget I'm suspect
number one.''

"The connection is not necessarily apparent." Antony
gave him a look in which interest, for the moment, seemed
uppermost. "However, I've said I'm sorry—really, I am!
—but I can't help you.''

"Why not?" George sounded belligerent.

"I have my living to earn, after all.''

"The firm are quite prepared——"

"The Bar Council——"

"You could arrange something," said Jenny, very quietly. Antony looked at her. "Couldn't you?" she insisted.

Antony turned away, and kicked again at the fire, and
remained staring down intently at the resultant blaze. Stephen found his expression enigmatic, and frowned George
into silence when the latter would have spoken. Maitland
said at last, "I could be free in a fortnight, with luck.
Would that do?" He looked up, caught the exchange of
glances, and grinned at George's look of bewilderment.
"You needn't feel obliged to me, either of you," he

pointed out gently. "I have an exaggerated bump of curiosity, as you may have guessed. Jenny humours me. That's all!"

And very pretty too, Stephen reflected. George seemed only too thankful to have got what he wanted, and didn't seem disposed to question the whys and wherefores. But he himself was as certain as he could be that Maitland's reluctance had been genuine; and that the reason for his capitulation, whatever it might be, was not the one he had given.

Jenny was sitting back now, and her face was in the shadow. He thought she was watching her husband, but her expression told him nothing. George was declaring his gratification in choice—though pompous—phrases. Antony lounged against the mantel, outwardly tranquil; yet there was tension in the room. Stephen deceived himself in considering himself untouched by what was going on, but he was right in thinking that the strain was something independent of his own feelings.

Maitland moved abruptly, and went back to his chair. George's gratitude trailed to a stop. "So we can think about our next move," he concluded ineffectually.

"Up to you!" Antony was unhelpful. But after a moment's uncomfortable silence he apparently relented. "Come now, the idea seems to be that I shall join the firm. Do I get myself taken on as a—a technical assistant?"

George regarded him pityingly. "My good ass, technical assistants have to know *some*thing."

"In fact," added Stephen, "it is a sad commentary on our profession that the higher you go, the less evidence of intelligence need you display in order to maintain your reputation."

"Well, I have thought about this, naturally," said George, apparently feeling that the ice had been broken. "Willie's always complaining he needs someone to read the small print on contracts."

"Who," said Antony, "is Willie?"

"Company Sec.," said George. "You'll like him."

"But can he, do you suppose, be induced to like me?"

"When he understands the position——"

"I see. Well, I'm in your hands."

And in saying that, thought Stephen, as they made their farewells half an hour later, Maitland had again been guilty in some degree of paltering with the truth. Complacent he might be, for the present and so long as it suited him; but resigned, as he said, to George's—or anybody else's—manipulation, very definitely not.

When Antony got upstairs again from seeing his visitors to the door, he found Jenny still sitting in her favourite corner of the sofa. He advanced to the hearth-rug and looked down at her quizzically. "Well?" he asked.

"You wanted to go, Antony; I couldn't bear you to refuse because of me. At least," she corrected herself, "you'd never have been happy if you'd turned them down."

"How well you know me, love! And, of course, you also know why." His tone was light; but to Jenny, who knew him so well, the undercurrent of bitterness was very evident.

"It's a job that needs doing," she said quietly. "And one that you can do."

Antony meditated this for a moment, and then grinned at her. "That's really neat," he approved. "Almost true and all the uncomfortable bits left out." Jenny met his eyes steadily, but her face was flushed, and after a moment he held out a hand to her. "I'm sorry, love, that wasn't fair. And I know you hate all this."

Jenny, protesting unconvincingly, could not bring herself to a direct denial.

CHAPTER THREE

THE MINISTRY moved with surprising speed; the unknown Mr. Akeroyd, it seemed, must be a gentleman of some determination. Antony, finding himself a temporary Civil Servant, professed to find some humour in the situation; but he went about his preparations for leaving chambers with a noticeable lack of cheerfulness, which was only partly caused by the necessity of returning a brief that had promised him the opportunity of arguing a fascinating point concerning the rights of copyholders which had never previously come his way.

Within the week there was a letter from General Aircraft, indecipherably signed by 'William Knowles, Secretary'; which referred to 'our recent meeting,' rambled briefly among National Insurance Cards and code numbers, and ended by engaging him, unequivocally, as Assistant Company Secretary, at a salary of £1,500 a year. There followed an interview with Milner, whose comments consisted mainly of a bitter series of complaints against 'these blasted industrialists.' "Think they've done it all when we've given them clearance for their bright lads," he grumbled. Antony, agreeing doubtfully, did not find him exhilarating company.

They drove north on a bleak Sunday in mid-December. It was fortunate that Jenny loved driving, as a war-time injury to his shoulder had made it, for her husband, so painful as to be almost impossible. This evening, however, she was secretly thankful when she turned the car between the tall stone pillars that marked the entrance to Holly Royd. George had promised accommodation in "a decent sort of guest-place,'' and she only hoped his judgment was to be trusted.

It was a tall, gaunt-looking house, and the woman who came to the door was tall, too, and had a grim way with her. Antony was unloading the luggage; Jenny, a little daunted, asked where she should put the car.

"There's room in shed, but leave it bide for now." Mrs. Ambler's tone was only a little less forbidding than her appearance, but her next words were encouraging. "You must be starved, the pair of you, but I've a good fire in your room." She turned, and beckoned imperiously to a young man who had appeared in the hall behind her. "You'd best be helping Mr. Maitland with his cases, Richard Appleby," she ordered. The young man, who was large and capable-looking, grinned amiably at Jenny, and disappeared into the darkness.

The hall was warm and bright, and smelled strongly of furniture polish. Mrs. Ambler led the way towards the stairs, and Jenny followed obediently. The room, on the first floor, had been described to her as a "double bed-sitter." The fire was cheerful; the wallpaper a distressing shade of green with a pattern of darker green cabbages; the serviceable linoleum had been polished till it shone dangerously, as did the furniture, though with less menace. There was a table with a red plush cloth, and curtains of the same material were drawn across the long windows. The bedspread was more modern, being one of the "Indian" designs that became popular in the twenties; the arm-chairs were hideously upholstered in brown leatherette, but looked comfortable. Jenny, aware of a certain unexpected anxiety in her hostess's manner, said fervently: "It's a lovely room," and looked round at the older woman, smiling.

"There now!" Mrs. Ambler was gratified, and relaxed a little of her austerity. "I didn't know but what you'd be expecting something grander," she confided. "You being from London, and that."

"I like this," said Jenny, positively.

"There now!" said her hostess again, and immediately became practical. "You'll not be going to Chapel tonight,

I expect, after coming all that way. Supper's at eight, so I'll just bring you up a nice pot of tea to warm you, before I go out.'' She made for the door, ignoring Jenny's protests (which indeed were half-hearted enough), and standing aside to let pass the two men, who had just arrived with the suitcases. Richard Appleby looked as though he might have been disposed to linger, but was taken firmly in tow by Mrs. Ambler, and departed reluctantly in her wake. Antony heaved the case he was carrying on to the bed, and looked about him with interest.

"I call this a bit of all right," he said at length. "Unless . . . can you live with the cabbages?''

"I can try," said Jenny. "Don't let's unpack yet, darling. We'll do it after tea."

"Supper is at eight," Antony informed her. "And Appleby looks well fed," he added hopefully.

"There's only one thing worrying me." Jenny dropped her coat untidily on to the bed, collapsed into one of the arm-chairs, and kicked off her shoes. She looked up at her husband. "Who's going to break it to Mrs. Ambler next Sunday that we aren't 'chapel'?" she asked.

They were still drinking tea from a large brown pot when there was a tap on the door; Antony went to open it, and Stephen Naylor came in. There was a trace of embarrassment in his greeting; Jenny cut short his apologies.

"Do you live here, too, Mr. Naylor? We saw Mr. Appleby as we came in; Antony says he works at General Aircraft.''

"Yes, there are six of us here altogether. Richard and I, and a chap called Vlasov, have rooms on this floor; and there are two lads from Sales, and another from Accounts upstairs." He grinned a little, though still rather sheepishly. "We've all got our orders to be on our best behaviour."

"Oh, dear!" said Jenny, and pulled a face at her husband.

"Vlasov," said Antony, and raised an inquiring eyebrow at the newcomer. "Sounds too good to be true," he added.

"Oh, Basil's all right. Family have been here for ever."

"I am glad to have your assurance, of course." Antony

permitted himself a little mild satire. "Your comments are *so* helpful."

Jenny looked anxious, but Stephen seemed to find the remark reasonable enough. "The point being, I suppose, that we're none of us 'all right' from your point of view?" he remarked, gloomily.

"Well, not at this stage," Antony agreed, amiably, and poured himself the last of the tea.

"But at least you can assume," said Stephen with more spirit, "that everyone concerned has a pretty good security rating."

"Yes, of course, I shan't forget that." He sounded thoughtful, and frowned a little as he spoke. "As for your improbably-named friend, is he one of your colleagues in Research?"

"He is."

"Working on this 'Full Moon' project?"

"Yes. Systems study. Not the stuff we had the trouble about . . . well, not directly."

"I see." He eyed the younger man speculatively. "Don't think me unwelcoming, Naylor, but is this a social call, or have you something to tell me?"

"Well . . . in a way."

Jenny got up, and began to move about the room quietly, finding hangers in the wardrobe, and starting to unpack. Stephen stared at the fire, apparently in no hurry to come to his point. Antony exchanged a glance with his wife, and settled himself comfortably in the chair she had vacated. "Expound," he said.

The other still hesitated. He drummed his fingers on the worn leatherette of the chair arm; felt in his pocket as though looking for cigarettes (but, evidently, he thought better of the idea); and said, at last, abruptly: "Something's up."

"For heaven's sake!" said Antony, exasperated. "What the hell do you think I'm doing here?"

If he expected a snarl in response he was the more mistaken. The flush on Stephen's face might have been a reflection of the firelight, but there could be no doubt of the mildness of his tone as he replied, "Something else, I mean."

"Well, what?"

"I don't know. At least," he added, as his host exclaimed impatiently, "there have been a lot of conferences, I *think* something went missing again, but I haven't been told."

"I see." Antony drew out the words thoughtfully. "Have you tackled George?"

"George has been . . . elusive." The admission, with its inference that he was in any way dependent on another man's opinion, was obviously one that Stephen found hard to make. "If I try to see him at work he always has someone with him."

Jenny was refolding a shirt, and again Antony caught her eye. She looked puzzled, but did not seem inclined to join in the conversation. He turned back to the visitor. "In that case, I don't see why you didn't tackle him at his home," he said.

"If you want it in words of one syllable," retorted Stephen, suddenly angry, "I did *try* to see him, but perhaps not as hard as I might have done. After all, if I had got a straight answer out of him, I don't expect I should have relished what he had to say."

"I see." He deliberated the advantages of further skirmishing, but decided that a direct line might prove more profitable. "But what do you think I can do about it?" he inquired.

"Nothing, I suppose. I can't think why I came to you." Stephen got up with one of his abrupt movements. "I'd better go," he said, and again he sounded angry.

Antony looked up at him with a glimmer of amusement. "I should sit down again, if I were you," he invited. "You came, I imagine, for the very human reason that you wanted to confide in somebody. You also hoped, no doubt, that I might later be able to provide you with the information you want." Stephen, who had gone back to his chair, but with an air of surprise at his own compliance, growled something under his breath and scowled at the fire. "Well, as to that I make no promises. How could I? But I shouldn't refine too much on George's attitude. He dearly loves a mystery.''

"I know all about George," said Stephen, positively. "He's got something up his sleeve, and I don't think I like it.''

"Well, I can't help you until I know more," Antony pointed out. "You'd better give me some details, now you're here.''

"Details?" said Stephen, cautiously. "What about?''

"Start with the missing letter," Antony replied. And he sounded more patient than he felt.

"Assuming that I'm telling the truth?" The bitterness was back in Stephen's voice. Antony replied without stopping to choose his words.

"Assuming—for the moment—that you're telling the truth." As he was coming to expect, this bluntness stimulated, rather than harassed, the other man. Naylor was giving the matter his consideration, and said at last:

"Well, Mickey, brought it over; she's a lass in the Secretary's office. I don't suppose she stayed in the lab for long. Bill signed for it . . . I was with Weston, I told you that. Bill put the envelope on my desk; Tom Burns saw him do that.''

"So we come to the question of opportunity.''

"Yes, I suppose so. I don't know——"

"You mentioned two men who knew the letter had come.''

"Harry Carleton. He works at the other side of the lab. And Evan Williams was with him.''

"Well . . . go on from there.''

"The lab's a busy place, you'll see for yourself. Pretty well any of the chaps could have walked through my section and been as invisible as Chesterton's postman.'' He paused, and looked at Antony directly. "George and Dick Appleby came over for a meeting," he added.

"I see." His tone was non-committal. "And that brings us to the night Bill Homer died.''

"That won't get you anywhere. Sergeant Billing told me he was the last to leave the lab, but anyone could have waited for him. And with the fog, no one could have told what cars were still on the car park."

"It was a really thick night?"

"You're thinking of an accident." Stephen's tone was accusing. Antony shrugged.

"Not necessarily. If a motive existed for killing him, it might have been chance that made that method possible. The real plan may have been quite different. Or there may have been a decoy. You can't tell."

"Two people?" There was a shocked incredulity in Stephen's voice that surprised both his companions. The veneer of worldly wisdom did not go very deep, it seemed. Or had this possibility opened up for him some new line of speculation? It seemed he intended to keep his thoughts to himself, for he met Antony's inquiring look with a blank one.

"Well, to get back to this question of opportunity——"

"I was out, if that's what you want to know," Stephen snapped. "It was turned eight when I left the lab. I might have waited for Bill, but I got the idea he didn't want me to. So I left him to it. Billing saw me leave; I didn't wait, but it took ages to get home and Mrs. Ambler had gone to choir practice, so I've no one to vouch for me, anyway."

"Your fellow-boarders?"

"Basil and Dick were out, too; but they often are. The others may have been in, but if so they were upstairs, I didn't see them." He paused, and then said as though with an effort, "There's one thing you might be interested to know. Harry Carleton has been dropping hints——"

"Well?" Antony prompted.

"Trying to stir up trouble, of course; he's the sort of chap who enjoys making you feel uncomfortable. Said he was there that night; over in admin., not in the lab. Said he was waiting outside for a lift, and found it 'interesting'."

"You feel he really knows something?"

"Yes, I do. I know it doesn't sound particularly convincing," said Stephen, angrily.

Antony waited a moment, to see if he had anything to add. "Very well, we'll leave it there." Stephen was eyeing him consideringly. "There is one other thing—" Naylor did not speak, but made a gesture which might be interpreted as indicating that he was resigned to whatever question might come. "How did you come to be part of the delegation?"

"I was talking to Josiah . . . I told him I'd resign if he wanted. *He* suggested I should go with George, I don't know why."

Antony thought he could make a guess about that, but doubted his companion would find much comfort in it. Josiah Akeroyd, it seemed, was alive to the advantage of having two messengers, one of whom could reliably be counted on as being a check on the other. "But George was hardly concerned," he said.

"Well, not directly. But he was in the lab that morning, I told you. As far as opportunity went——"

"That," said Antony slowly, "opens up a new train of thought." Stephen stared at him, and seeing the look he added irritably: "No, I don't mean anything by that remark, nothing more than I say."

Stephen stayed a few minutes longer, and they went over—abortively—the tale that had already been told. It was evident that there was too much going and coming in the laboratory for any very reliable evidence to be produced; while as for the night of the fog, all normal routine had been disrupted. The younger man grew restless under questioning, and made a poor hand at concealing his irritation. Jenny finished stowing away their belongings, and pushed the empty suitcases side by side into the corner. She came to sit on the arm of her husband's chair, and after a while Stephen got up and said in his abrupt way, "Thanks for bearing with me. I'll see you at supper. And if you want a lift to Carcroft in the morning, Maitland, I'll be glad to take you."

Antony accepted the offer, and looked thoughtful as the door closed and they heard Naylor's steps retreating across the landing. "I wonder why he came."

"You were probably right about his reasons." Jenny took possession of the chair their visitor had vacated, and sank into it with an exaggerated air of well-being.

"Perhaps I was. But he had it mighty pat about George's

opportunity. Was that pique? Or deliberate policy? Or was he just saying what came into his head?''

"I don't know," said Jenny. She sat up straight again, and looked at him with eyes that were suddenly troubled. "You can't *know* things like that," she said.

Antony looked at her with amused affection. "You can have a jolly good try," he pointed out.

Jenny wriggled uneasily. "But it's different, wondering about people, when you know them," she said.

"My dear child, you can't do this sort of job without 'knowing' the people concerned." Jenny pulled a face at him.

"Don't be so patronising." The protest was a half-hearted one, and she returned at once to her problem. "Is it always like this?" she asked.

"I'm afraid so. Are you going to hate it? You shouldn't have come."

"That," said Jenny, "would have been Much Worse." She looked into the fire, and she sighed a little. "But—oh, dear!—I wish one didn't like people."

CHAPTER FOUR

THEY WERE LATER than might have been expected, leaving for work next morning, but none of Antony's companions seemed unduly disturbed by the circumstance. Stephen drove an ancient Austin, which stormed the hills gallantly enough. The newcomer found himself supplied with a front seat and a running commentary on points of local interest. The other two passengers were the helpful Mr. Appleby, and a sad-eyed, soft-voiced young man who had been introduced only as "Basil." He had been absent from Sunday supper, and from the breakfast-table too; arriving only after repeated and loud-voiced adjurations from his colleagues, to take his place in the car with no appearance of haste, and with a sleepy smile at Antony by way of acknowledgement of Stephen's muttered introduction. It seemed likely that he was the improbably-named Mr. Vlasov, and Antony took what opportunity he could to study him when Stephen paused for a moment in his deliberately casual commentary, and he could twist round in his seat the better to listen to some eager questions from Dick Appleby on the subject of sport.

By contrast with his companion, who was large and muscular and craggy of countenance, Basil gave an impression of fragility which was probably misleading. Though more slightly built than Dick, he was also plumper; the lines of his face blurred a little, indeterminate. He was obviously disinclined for conversation, and as Appleby took this cheerfully for granted it was probably his usual form.

They stopped climbing at last, and the houses thinned out. On the right was a brick building, new and raw;

behind it the massive, steel-girdered works looked strangely impermanent. They turned in between stone gate-posts; well-kept gravel swept round to an old, grey house. A few frost-nipped chrysanthemums still straggled under the long windows. As the car drew up nothing was visible of the works behind the house, but as Antony opened the car door the noise met him, loud, insistent.

Stephen put down his window to give some last minute directions. "Through the main door here, the commission-aire will tell you." He had been hiding his anxiety well enough, but his voice was strained as he added: "I'll see you at lunch-time, most likely. If not, I'll give you a ring before we leave."

Whatever Antony Maitland might have possessed of natural diffidence, the life he had led had done nothing whatever to encourage its display, and very little to promote indulgence in so unprofitable an emotion. None the less, he was consious of some qualms as he watched the car drive away, a feeling of apprehension as disagreeable as it was unfamiliar. He was out of his element here, though perhaps not yet out of his depth. And the nostalgia he felt for the familiar things, for the bizarre outline of the Law Courts, for the sound and smell of the Strand, was for the moment uncomfortably intense.

There was a neat brass plate beside the door, proclaiming the registered offices of General Aircraft Limited. The threshold was well-whitened, the knocker and the massive handle had been polished until they shone with dazzling splendour. He paused a moment more, because here was the brink, here he must take the final step into the unknown: certainly into ways which were strange to him, but perhaps also to the boredom and the excitement which had once been a familiar part of life, to treachery, and hate and fear.

It was quieter inside, and the hall was warm and well-lit; from a counter which had been built across the back a tall man in the uniform of the Corps of Com-missionaires came forward. He was grey-haired, and had a fine moustache. "Can I help you, sir?"

"My name's Maitland. I believe Mr. Knowles is expecting me."

"Why, yes, Mr. Maitland, sir. I'll just let him know you're here." He turned with his hand on the telephone and smiled at the newcomer. "I'm Ambler, sir. It's my missus runs Holly Royd." He picked up the phone as he spoke, so no reply seemed called for, and when he had delivered his message he went on in the same unhurried, but persistent way: "That's it, sir. Straight up the stairs, and the first door on the right. I'd show you, sir, but being on my own at the moment I can't leave the desk. I'll not need to give you a badge; you'll be getting a pass, being staff, as I understand from Mrs. A. And I hope your good lady will be finding things comfortable; proper taken a fancy to her, the missus has."

So much, reflected Antony as he made for the staircase, for the taciturn Yorkshireman! The Army had doubtless taken Ambler about the world a little, but it had not succeeded either in curbing his speech or in accelerating his movements. He wondered idly as he went whether Mrs. Ambler had in her time also followed the drum. As he paused for a moment on the landing Ambler's voice came up to him from the hall below.

"First on the right, sir. Go straight in, Mr. Knowles is waiting for you." Antony found the door, tapped lightly, and entered on the summons.

It was a big room, a little bare perhaps, because the desk had been pushed near the window into a position which was obviously not the one a regard for symmetry would have dictated. There was a fire in the grate, an old-fashioned Turkey carpet, two leather chairs and several straight-backed ones, a bookcase with one door ajar and the contents not too orderly. Antony stood just inside the door to make his observations, and then turned his attention to the man who got up from the desk to greet him.

William Knowles, the Company Secretary, was a man in his late forties; dark-haired, not over tall, with a bird-like brightness of eye and a boisterous laugh. He greeted Antony warmly, waved him to a chair by the fire, and disappeared momentarily through another door at the side of the room; Antony could hear him in animated converse with someone in the room beyond.

"Maitland's here, Miss Jenner. See we're not disturbed, there's a good girl . . . well, not unless you *have* to. Coffee about ten o'clock, because I'm seeing Sir Thomas at half past . . . and tell Mickey I need some more cigarettes . . . oh, well, if you really think I ought to, but I shan't have time until this afternoon, you know." He came back clutching a bulky file which he dumped on the desk and covered promptly with a sprinkling of papers. "May as well be comfortable," he remarked, and threw himself down in the chair across the hearth from his visitor. "So you're our new Assistant Secretary," he said; and grinned.

There didn't seem to be any answer to that except "Yes."

"I gather I engaged you at an interview when I was in London a month ago. Miss Jenner won't forgive me in a hurry for forgetting to tell her at the time."

"I'm afraid," said Antony, "I haven't much idea what I'm supposed to do."

"Don't worry about that, dear boy." He added, wistfully, "as a matter of fact, your background is just what you've always wanted. The legal stuff takes altogether too much of my time, so nobody will be at all surprised at our being here. Of course, too many people knew we hadn't been advertising, but I got over that all right." He paused, eyeing the younger man with his head a little on one side, his expression at once hopeful and amused. "I had a talk with George, and then let it be understood I'd taken on the nephew of an old friend."

"Well, I suppose——" (But, after all, he thought, it was a very minor complication.) "Er—who——?"

"Watson. The Stock-Exchange chap. I *do* know him, as a matter of fact, and he is your uncle, isn't he?"

"Near enough," said Antony. "To be exact, *my* wife is *his* wife's niece. I doubt if he'd recommend me for a job, though. He's quite a good sort, but Aunt Carry's a holy terror."

"Well, I didn't ask him, of course." Knowles's smile was both self-satisfied and engaging. "Merely artistic verisimilitude——"

"And they're both over two hundred miles away!"

"Exactly! Now, did my letter tell you everything? Your security clearance has come through, so there'll be no difficulty there."

"There's one point that's rather important," said Antony. "Who, besides yourself, knows my real position?"

"Akeroyd, of course; and George, and Stephen Naylor. Besides them, only myself and Sir Thomas. We haven't been anxious to make the matter public."

"No, I'm sure . . . but—you'll have to start from the beginning, I'm afraid—Sir Thomas is your Managing Director, isn't he? Sir Thomas Overbury?" He paused, with an inquiring look at his companion. "Comment perhaps, is not in order?"

"Most emphatically not." Knowles affected a serious look. "I gather you're a student of history, or perhaps of famous trials. But, like Queen Victoria, we don't find the subject amusing."

"I'll remember."

"Good." He nodded his approval, and added reflectively: "Sir Thomas is an unusually capable man, not a doubt of that——" (he seemed to be picking his words) "—so perhaps we should grant him his foibles." He grinned apologetically. "As they say in these parts, 'there's nowt so queer as folk'."

"George said," remarked Antony, "that the Chief Engineer—Mr. Akeroyd, isn't it?—was inclined to eccentricity."

"Now, I call that too bad of George." Knowles seemed, for the moment, genuinely put out. "There's nothing wrong with Josiah but that he says what he thinks. Of course," he added, pensively, "you might say his ideas aren't always exactly orthodox. You'll be thinking we're an odd bunch," he challenged.

"I'll reserve judgment," said Antony. The other man eyed him in silence for a moment, and then said with apparent irrelevance:

"Y'know, Maitland, it's interesting to meet you. Instructive, really. We had a chap in your line here one day—security, I mean; one of the Ministry boys—can't say he impressed me much, didn't seem to know his way about very well, and left his brief-case in the office when he went. As for you, now, if I didn't know why you're here I swear I'd take you at face value."

"Well, you see, sir," said Antony, with no change of manner other than a little, added earnestness, "it's all strange ground, but I'm very anxious to get on well. It isn't easy, making your way at the Bar these days——"

Knowles stared at him, and then threw back his head and laughed. "You'll do!" he said, after a moment. (His laughter was infectious, and Antony found himself grinning, too.) "But I ought to warn you," he added seriously, "you're not going to find it easy."

"I don't expect to. We'd hardly have indulged in this elaborate set-up——"

"I don't mean that. I mean, you'll meet some opposition——"

Not Akeroyd, who had made the original suggestion; not George, or Stephen, not openly at least; not—surely? —this friendly, helpful man. "Sir Thomas?" he inquired.

"He was not exactly pleased with the arrangement," admitted Knowles. "He said we'd no proof that anything was needed."

"And you haven't, of course. He's quite right."

"Proof? Well, I suppose not. But I'm worried, Maitland."

"Something else has happened." Consciously, or unconsciously, he echoed Stephen's statement of the night before. "You'd better tell me."

William Knowles's manner had changed now. He said uneasily: "It may be nothing——"

Antony repressed his impatience. "Tell me about it," he repeated.

"One of our chaps in Missile Research—a group leader working on the Full Moon hydraulics—hasn't shown up the last three days. He hasn't been home, either. That's five days he's been missing, counting the week-end."

"How seriously would you take that—if it weren't for the other things?"

"How can I tell?" His tone held a shade of petulance. "The other things have happened."

"You know the man concerned. Was he married? Was he reliable, as a worker, as a husband? What was his salary, his commitments?" He added encouragingly, as Knowles seemed to be hesitating: "I only want an opinion."

"His name is Harry Carleton; he's married, no children yet." Knowles sounded troubled. "He's sound technically, but not brilliant—I'm quoting, of course. I've heard he's been in financial difficulties once or twice; something about borrowing money, I'm the last person who'd hear details, you know. Salary £1,250; no house purchase, not through the company anyway; they nearly all run cars, his is a Morris, neither very new nor very large. From his Income Tax coding I should say he'd no dependents other than his wife."

And that seemed pretty comprehensive. And Stephen had said Harry Carleton had been trying to stir up trouble. "What happened?" Antony asked.

"He went home to supper last Tuesday, and then came back to the lab for some reason. I don't know quite how long he stayed (for obvious reasons, we can't ask too many questions), but he didn't go home that night. His wife doesn't seem to have been too worried (don't know if that means anything); he was due to go down to London the next morning, anyway. We never missed him until Mrs. Carleton rang Miss Jenner on Thursday, then we made some inquiries, and found he'd never gone to see Knight after all."

"But you kept the matter to yourselves?"

"Well, yes, we had to. Unless we wanted to start a hue and cry."

"Precisely. But why not? I know all about harmful publicity, but this seems dangerously like insanity."

"My dear boy, think of it . . . the police——"

"I'm not talking about the police."

"I assure you," said Knowles, unhappily, shifting his ground, "I made the strongest representations." Antony, who had been scowling into the fire, looked at him and grinned sympathetically.

"Am I to understand this Sir Thomas of yours is a difficult man to deal with?"

Knowles spread his hands. "Pig-headed!" he said. "But, in fairness, the decision was his to make."

"Then I must take it up with him."

The other shook his head. "It won't be the slightest use," he mourned. "Wasting your time, dear boy!"

"Well, we'll see," said Antony, who found this form of address unnerving. "Meanwhile, what do you think about this—Carleton, was it?—about his disappearance?"

"It could be coincidence . . . people *do* disappear, for domestic or financial reasons; there's nothing in what I know of him to make it unlikely."

"So the matter has been kept between the same group of people?"

"Except that Stephen Naylor was not informed of it."

"Why was that?" Knowles gave him a blank look, and he added without much doubt that his guess was the right one: "Sir Thomas again?"

"He had reason, I think." He was on the defensive now. "The previous occurrences seemed, after all, to centre on the work Naylor was doing. Besides, he was here that Tuesday evening . . . the night Carleton didn't go home."

Antony ignored him. He said reflectively: "The more I hear of Sir Thomas, the more I feel that we aren't exactly soul-mates."

"Well, I must rely on your discretion." Suddenly Knowles seemed at ease again, with no more than a gentle amusement in the conversation. "Don't misunderstand me, Maitland. He's a very able man, a great asset to the company. But I felt some measure of—er—extraordinary frankness was due to you——"

"Don't worry. I won't expect a red carpet." Antony, in his turn, had reverted to the quiet note on which the interview had begun. "But perhaps I'd better get down to work."

"I'm a little at a loss; what do you want to do first?"

"Forget for a moment that I'm a fake. If I were really your assistant, what would you give me to do?"

"I should give you that file," said the other, rising with alacrity, "and that letter from an Indian Government Department (it's not bad value, really, their idea of English as she is spoke); oh, and that Agency Agreement——"

Antony got up. "Something," he suggested, "to take me down to the laboratory."

"Missiles? Well, yes, of course. There's a letter from the Ministry——" He was looking in the fullest of the filing baskets on his desk as he spoke, and a moment later produced some closely-typed sheets of foolscap and waved them at his companion in a pleased way. "It's really self-explanatory," he added. "I could let Accounts take it up, but they're only interested in the money angle, not in what we're contracting to do. If you talk to Weston——"

"Yes, I see," said Antony, untruthfully, five minutes later. His mind was completely befuddled with incomprehensible facts. "That sounds like enough to keep me amused," he added. "Where do you want me to work?"

"There's a little room across the landing. It's very small, I'm afraid. We've put a desk there for you." Knowles—watching the files pass out of his possession—had the air of one who propitiates the Goddess Chance by making no mention of her favours. He glanced at his watch, and moved towards the door to the other office. "I'll introduce you to the girls first; they'll give you some coffee, I expect, and show you where everything is. I know Josiah wants to see you as soon as possible, but he won't be in till noon."

"I can hardly wait," murmured Antony, following. Knowles grinned at him over his shoulder.

It was another large room, though not quite large enough for the clutter of filing cabinets, and two big desks. At the far end a slightly-built girl with straight red-gold hair had spread her papers along the top of the files and was sorting them industriously. At the desk nearer the door a tall, dark girl put down the telephone and turned towards them eagerly. Her hair was curly, and very untidy. She said, without ceremony: "Well, thank goodness!"

Knowles did not seem unduly perturbed by this greeting. "This is Mr. Maitland," he said, waving a proprietory hand. "Miss Jenner, Maitland, who knows everything. And the little one is Mickey, who knows the rest of it."

Miss Jenner gave him a friendly look, but her attention was obviously elsewhere. Mickey, turning, revealed that in addition to red-gold hair she had a snub nose and an engaging smile. Knowles, seeing his secretary simmering gently with suppressed information, abandoned the formalities and gave her his attention. "All right, Miss Jenner. Out with it!"

She waved a hand towards the telephone. "That," she said, rather as though it were a personal enemy, "that was Mr. Williams. He wants to see you."

"Urgent?"

"It is, indeed." Her voice had for a moment a lilt which was presumably an echo of the importunate Mr. Williams. "I told him he could *try* at twelve o'clock."

"What does he want?"

"He didn't say. Before that there was Miss Macaulay, about those figures Sir Thomas wants; he said Monday would do, but of course—ten o'clock isn't soon enough! Mickey's sorting them now."

"Then that's all right."

"And Cashiers' rang up because Mr. Daly's last expense sheet doesn't add up right; I said I'd tell Miss Brewster. And Sales rang up for your list of Christmas presents, and did you know you mustn't send anything to the Ministry people that doesn't have the firm's name on it? And Mr. Barton was looking for you, because the Ministry *still* haven't sent that progress payment. And Mr. Grant says one of the Christmas Club treasurers in the works has spent the doings, and what should he do about it? I tried to persuade him to use his discretion, but I bet he waits for you. And Mr. Knight's secretary rang to say he couldn't manage the 18th after all, and wouldn't after Christmas do for the Board Meeting?'' She paused for breath, and Mickey added, looking up again from her task:

"And Mr. Weston wanted to know when Mr. Carleton would be back. I said we didn't know."

"Well, that's good. Let's see now: I'll take Sir Thomas's estimates when I go in at half past ten; you've made Chashiers' and Sales Department happy—if anything *could* content Cashiers'," he added, doubtfully. "Tell Mr. Barton to get on to old hatchet face; he can say our suppliers are threatening to stop delivery if they don't get something on account. It isn't true, but it sounds better than if *we* threaten to do so. If the Board Meeting's postponed, that's all to the good, isn't it? So that only leaves poor Evan's crisis and the bereaved Christmas Club members. Tell Grant to come up, will you?'' He smiled amiably at Antony, rather as though he had forgotten who he was, and vanished back into his own room again. Miss Jenner threw her note-book on the desk and turned again to the telephone; Mickey stacked the last of her papers together and banged a staple into the corner of the pile. "And now," she said, with an encouraging look in Antony's direction, "we'll have some coffee."

The older girl turned from the phone again; evidently Mr. Grant had not been far to seek. "Do you want me to show you your room, Mr. Maitland?''

"He's going to have some coffee first," said Mickey positively. She produced a kettle as if by magic from the bottom drawer of one of the filing cabinets, and made for the door. "Don't bully him, Susie!''

Susie Jenner paused for the first time to look at the newcomer, who looked back at her with an air of apology which was not altogether assumed. "I'm afraid I'm going to be an awful nuisance to you," he said.

"I expect we shall bear it." She had a direct look, and an air of unassuming competence which pleased him. (In fact, he thought, she and her employer were well matched; their conversation together had had a false air of frenzy, but in fact all points had been covered—and without loss of time.) "Are you just being polite," she added. "Or is it really strange . . . all this?''

"It's really strange."

"Well, I hope you won't find it dull." She sounded doubtful. "There's not much glamour about industry, I'm afraid."

"And precious little about the law." He looked rueful. "Even when you're lucky enough to get a brief." It seemed most artistic to stop at that point, no good going too far out of character; and he seemed to have achieved his effect, for Susie gave a small warning frown at the younger girl, who had made a tempestuous re-entrance with a kettle that was obviously over full. Mickey's skirt swirled about her as she went down on her knees to plug it in, in an out-of-the-way corner; a moment later she came to her feet gracefully, saying as she did so:

"Oh, well, it's not so bad here, after all." She was taking cups from the same drawer which had housed the kettle; Antony strolled to the window, and looked across at yet another brick building which reared itself incongruously heavenwards about twenty yards away. Susie picked up her pen, put it down again, and folded her hands together on her blotting-pad. "Have you met Sir Thomas yet?" she inquired.

As she spoke Antony had an impression that the question was not asked idly, that—perhaps?—she knew something; and, after all, if the Managing Director's protests had been as vehement as Knowles maintained, what was more likely than that some at least of his indignation was common knowledge? He wondered a little uneasily how far this went, but after all she seemed discreet enough, this quiet, pleasant girl; and even Mickey, with her more scatterbrained ways, did not strike him as untrustworthy. All the same . . .

"No, I haven't met him," he said. "I gather he's quite a chap."

"Well——" Susie seemed to be considering the point. "He's a very clever man——"

"But not nearly so clever as he thinks he is," said Mickey. Her preparations were proceeding with careful speed. "He isn't good at *people*," she added, by way of explanation. But she glanced as she spoke at the older girl, as though trying to judge her reaction.

"No, he isn't." This seemed to be safer ground, but there was still an air of caution about Susie's remarks. "And as for the technical appointments——"

"You'd think he'd leave them to Josiah," Mickey agreed. She looked across at Antony with her friendly grin. "The fact is," she confided, "we'd make a pretty good job of running things here . . . if only they'd leave it to us."

CHAPTER FIVE

ABOUT HALF AN HOUR later, fortified by two cups of coffee and ten minutes' unrewarding study of the "self-explanatory" document, Antony took advantage of Mickey's routine trip with the classified letters to claim her escort to the Missile Division. "You'd better see Mr. Weston," said Susie Jenner, glancing knowledgeably at the letter in his hand; and again frowned warningly at the younger girl who seemed, in her impulsive way, to be about to add something to this advice.

They left the old house by the back way, passed between two of the tall red brick buildings which made so incongruous a frame-work for its solidity, and came to a high wire fence. The commissionaire on duty eyed Mickey indulgently, and upon her introduction waved aside the pass that her companion was dutifully offering. "Miss Carmichael will look after you, sir," he said encouragingly, as he swung the gate open. "But you'll soon learn your way about." Antony, with a depressed feeling that he must be looking as lost as he felt, followed his guide across a wide strip of gravel to a low, wooden building.

Inside there was a narrow corridor, with a row of offices along one side. . . . "Chief of Research" . . . "Chief Development Engineer" . . . "Systems Study" . . . "U.K. Trials." The first door stood open. "I expect he's in the lab," said Mickey, hardly pausing to note that the occupant was missing. She went on quickly down the passage, and pushed open the swing door that led into the main laboratory.

Antony, not usually at a loss for words, found it difficult to convey to Jenny later any clear impression of the ordered confusion the scene presented. Presumably some guiding hand had ordained the lay-out of the benches; to an outsider it seemed purely fortuitous, a labyrinth created by a madman. On all sides, it seemed, technicians were bending solicitously over incredible birds'-nests of wire and what he was to learn to think of as components. On each bench needles moved across dials, lights flashed, and a bewildering array of equipment was in operation . . . a very devil's dance, and not without its own fascination. An elderly man in one corner was peering entranced at a small piece of metal swinging on the end of a string; from time to time he consulted a stop-watch anxiously, and noted something on a pad.

From this scene of comparative calm, Antony's eye was caught by a heavy frame with a spike sticking out of the bottom. This unlikely-looking contraption was suspended over a wire enclosure, and was at the moment being wound up towards the ceiling, thirty feet above. As he watched, a button was pressed, and the frame hurtled downwards, so that the spike buried itself deeply in a block of lead. "It's a way of subjecting equipment to the kind of shocks it will experience in flight," said Basil Vlasov, at his elbow. Maitland, who had momentarily lost himself, turned with a start.

"The kind of thing no home should be without," he murmured; and added, vaguely, "I'm told I want Mr. Weston." Mickey said, by way of explanation:

"He isn't in his office."

"He *was* in environmental testing," said Basil. "We'll have a look."

"Thanks." He paused a moment, staring in a fascinated way at the spike, which had now started again its laboured ascent. Mickey said, "See you later," and made off purposefully. Antony followed his new guide in the opposite direction.

A high-pitched whine was coming from one of the rooms leading off the lab; inside, delicate looking pieces of electronic gear were being vibrated by machines that looked to the uninstructed eye nothing more nor less than enormous loud speakers, but with electrical equipment occupying the position where the cone would normally have been. The gentlemen presiding over this scene of destruction wore pleased expressions, but apparently Richard Weston was not among them.

They ran him to earth presently outside the computer room: a dapper man of middle height, who greeted Basil almost affectionately, and turned upon his new acquaintance, as the introduction was made, a smile of quite unnecessary cordiality. Antony began to expound his mission, uneasily earnest.

The explanation was not allowed to proceed very far. Weston began to fidget, and glanced at his watch. "Yes, well, of course," he said. "I can't stop now, but Basil here can tell you . . . it's an urgent matter, old man," he added, turning to his colleague. "Got to keep the Ministry happy, you do see that, don't you?" He took himself off, still talking. Antony glanced inquiringly at his companion, whose expression of rather lazy complaisance had not varied.

"And you know what *that* means," said Stephen's voice behind him. "He hasn't the faintest idea what it's all about. I wonder you can stand it, Basil."

Vlasov did not answer this directly, but smiled absently at each of his companions in turn. "You might care to look around a bit," he suggested to Antony. "Unless you're in a hurry."

"I'm sure it would be most useful." He was staring around him as he spoke, and did not need to simulate an air of bewilderment. "I've never seen anything like it before," he added.

"In that case," said Stephen, "you'd better meet GADA." He backed through the doorway behind him, and waved a proprietorial hand. "General Aircraft Differential Analyser," he explained. Antony followed him, wondering as he went what etiquette dictated by way of acknowledgment of such an introduction.

It was a small room, and it seemed that the computer must have grown in size beyond its original conception. Maitland's first startled conviction that a Laocoon-like struggle was taking place between the machine and its attendant quickly gave way to a more ordered impression. The young man in the shabby sports jacket was merely making a note by hand on one of the wide paper streamers which the machine, a moment before, had been rolling out. He took no notice at all of their entrance, but walked back to the console and began to press what appeared to be a random selection of knobs. Lights flashed, and the streamers began to emerge again. At the side of the room an older man, equally preoccupied, was sitting in a sort of nest of used paper, doing something with a slide-rule. "Er—*most* impressive," said Antony, and met Stephen's eye with a look that was faintly apologetic.

"Nothing of the sort," said Basil. He spoke languidly, as though the effort were almost too much for him. "A snare and a delusion . . . no more, no less."

"Now, look here," said Stephen, belligerently. "I know we had that spot of trouble last week——"

"Moloch," said Basil, dreamily. He considered the comparison, and apparently found it satisfactory. "Its capacity for ingesting valuable information without producing any results at all must be quite unequalled." Stephen grinned reluctantly.

"Well . . . all right!" he said. "But I haven't noticed much progress——"

"My colleagues are harassed," the other man conceded. "They cannot see that all we need is a little patience. And the joke is," he added, a few minutes later, conducting Maitland through a sound-proof room where rows of girls with calculating machines are noisily tapping out figures, "the joke is, when all *this* is collated, the results will undoubtedly horrify them still further."

But once in his office the problem raised by the Ministry's letter was quickly settled, and explained with a clarity for which Antony, in his capacity as Assistant Company Secretary, should certainly have been grateful. Vlasov, it seemed, for all his sleepy air, was both clear-headed and competent; an impression which his unbusinesslike appearance in a wine-coloured corduroy jacket did nothing to foster. Antony, maintaining his rather worried look, ventured a question about Richard Weston's place in the technical hierarchy.

"Chief of Research," said the other promptly. "This group of mine comes under him—Systems Study, that is—and Stephen's computer group, and Propulsive Methods, and Advance Projects——" He caught his companion's eye, and smiled gently. "Yes . . . I'm sorry. It *is* confusing, but you'll get used to us in time."

"I suppose so." There was no confidence in Antony's tone. "But you were telling me . . . do you mean Weston is the head of the Missile Division?"

"Well, not exactly. To begin with, he comes under Josiah, you know. *He*'s Technical Director, and of course his interests are wider than just our affairs. Then there's John Lund; Chief Development Engineer, Richard's opposite number really. I mean, if you look at that family tree Willie's got tucked away somewhere you'll find them on the same level. And, come to think of it, you may as well meet John while you're over here. It may be useful——"

They went out into the long passage. Weston's office still seemed to be empty, but the adjoining room—whose door also stood open—showed plenty of signs of life. Following obediently in Basil's wake, Antony paused on the threshold to sort out his ideas; the odd thing was, no one seemed to stay in the same place for two minutes together, and how anything ever got done . . .

But at least, it seemed, the man sitting at the desk in the large, under-furnished room was the man Basil expected to find there. John Lund was a tall man, who wore his tweeds with distinction, and his authority with humorous ease. His companion, Evan Williams, was half a head shorter, with a heavy pair of shoulders and an excitable air; he paused in his harangue only long enough to acknowledge the introductions Basil made without actual rudeness, and then returned to his point.

"Tell me this, then, John, does security come under Willie Knowles's office now, or doesn't it?"

"It does, of course," said Lund. He exchanged a glance with Basil, half weary, half amused. "But I don't see what else he could have said, you know."

"The matter must be investigated," said Williams. "And so I shall tell him." There was the true Welsh lilt in his voice, which made his most commonplace words almost musical. "Someone has been tampering with my papers, there is no mistake about that."

"But Evan, anyone might have been in your office and taken a look at what was on your desk——" Lund's tone was, perhaps, too elaborately reasonable, and the other man's indignation was made apparent in every line of his body.

"That is what Knowles said, and I do not find it very funny. I had been looking at results of the stability runs Bill did, but there was no call for someone to be looking in my files and in my brief-case."

"No, I see." John Lund looked startled now, and again he looked at Basil. "I take it you're sure . . . yes, of course!"

Basil had sunk into a chair near the window and closed his eyes as though it was too much effort to give the matter his whole attention. He opened them now, and said in his quiet way: "Well, Evan, here's the man you want. Perhaps you can persuade Maitland to take you seriously."

"There is no need for all this fuss." Lund spoke decisively. "Obviously Knowles has got to think things over."

"I don't quite understand," said Antony, hesitantly. "What is the trouble, and what could I do about it?" He could not have complained that they ignored his question; they all answered him at once.

"It's a matter of security——"

"It may seem odd, but security is the Secretary's responsibility——"

"Basil thinks, as Knowles's assistant, you might be able——"

"There is the question," said Antony, addressing his reply to Williams, "of what exactly you want to be done about it." Evan opened his mouth to reply, and then thought better of it.

"Yes, it is awkward, isn't it?" said Basil, for the moment almost animated.

Williams said angrily: "I shall take my own precautions, you may be sure of that.'' And a moment later the door banged upon what Antony felt certain was a characteristically tempestuous exit.

Lund leaned back with a relieved sigh, and looked at the newcomer with a blend of gratitude and amusement. ''That was sheer genius,'' he said. ''Did you know?''

''I just thought——'' said Antony, and allowed the sentence to trail into incoherence. He did not look, at that moment, at all likely to have said anything useful, except perhaps by accident; he was thinking that neither of his companions was a particularly easy man to deceive, and that he didn't trust either of them an inch.

''The thing is,'' said Lund confidentially, ''he's excitable. Speaks without thinking.'' As the understatement of the week, Antony felt this could hardly have been bettered.) ''And ten to one it's all imagination, you can't expect Willie to start leaping about——''

As though the words had been a cue, the door burst open again, and George Ramsey shot in unceremoniously. He spent perhaps three seconds on the conventions; Antony gathered from his rather offhand greeting that their acquaintance was acknowledged and George, perhaps, was claiming some credit for his introduction to the firm. When this had been done he turned to Lund accusingly.

''Look here, John, this business of the hydraulics is getting serious.''

''Yes,'' said Lund. He sounded resigned, but not especially worried. ''As soon as Harry gets back——''

''But when will that be?'' George's voice went up on the query, and he looked around at the other men, as though seeking their sympathy. ''I've been talking to Kershaw——''

''Who,'' said Basil, ''is Kershaw?''

''Toolmaker,'' replied George, briefly.

''And what's his trouble?''

''I told you.'' Ramsey produced the words explosively. ''It's the whole design. He says it calls for an impossible degree of accuracy.''

''Did he really say that?'' said Basil, waking up again.

''Well, perhaps not that exactly. But, dammit, he's a

highly experienced chap." He paused, and again looked from one of his colleagues to the other. "Look here, haven't you heard *any*thing from Harry?" he asked.

"Not so far." For the first time it seemed to strike Lund that the conversation might be puzzling to an outsider. He looked at Antony with a vague air of apology and explained: "It's one of our chaps, Harry Carleton, who hasn't been in for a day or two."

"He hasn't been home either," said Ramsey. Lund made a sudden movement with his hands, and picked up the paper-knife from his desk and began to stab with it at the blotting-pad. Antony had the impression he had been about to protest at this bluntness, and had thought better of the impulse. "And Linda's pretty worried," George went on. "I can tell you that."

"So I should suppose."

"But not worried enough to do anything about it," said Basil. "And, after all, it's nearly a week."

"The M.D. was most anxious——"

"Yes, well, I'll try to see him this afternoon." Lund's tone was decisive, suddenly; the statement obviously intended as a dismissal. "I'm not at all sure he's right in his opinion."

Basil got up, and drifted towards the door. "I'm damned sure he's wrong," he said. "But do you really think you can get him to change his mind?"

Antony was still pondering the character of the Managing Director, as revealed by this exchange, when he got back at last to his own quarters. He was aware of curiosity, and did not know how quickly it was to be satisfied. He had gone into the big office and was discussing the question of stationery supplies with Mickey when a buzzer sounded and a red light glowed in the box-like contraption on Susie's desk. She flicked a switch, and spoke conversationally. "Yes, Sir Thomas?"

The voice that replied was clear and a little over-loud; the harshness might have been inherent, or due perhaps to a slight distortion from the machine. "Maitland with you, Miss Jenner? I want him right away."

"Yes, he's here, Sir Thomas. I'll tell him." She flicked the key again, and looked up at Antony. "Can you go across now, Mr. Maitland?" Her eyes told him no more than did her voice, but again he had the impression of hidden knowledge.

He glanced at his watch, and found it was still a few minutes before noon. "Mr. Knowles——?" he said, tentatively.

"Don't wait for anything," advised Mickey. "I'll show you," she offered, making for the door. Antony exchanged a smile with Susie Jenner, and followed with a sudden feeling of helplessness; he had an impression which did not please him, of being taken by the current. Mickey's heels clicked ahead of him on the parquet floor. "That's Miss Macaulay's room," she hissed, indicating a closed door at the other side of the landing. "The thing is to go through her, unless he sends for you direct." She paused by another, wider doorway, knocked and stepped aside. Antony said, "thank you," mechanically, a forthright voice invited him, and he pushed open the door.

The room lay across the front of the house, and was full of sunlight; the sun was low on this December day, so that it shone full in his eyes and blinded him for a moment. Two sturdy figures, dimly seen, got up as he closed the door again: the forthright voice spoke from behind the desk and he turned towards it blindly, lifting his left hand to shield his eyes.

"This is our Assistant Secretary, gentlemen," said the voice. It held a note of satisfaction, perhaps even of malice. "As our legal expert he seems the man to deal with this little matter. Sergeant Murray and Constable Gill, Maitland," the voice went on. "Of the local police."

The taller of the two figures moved; there was the rattle of a blind, a moment's fumbling before the slats fell into place. Antony dropped his hand; he could see his companions now, though still through a reddish haze: two big men in uniform. And seated at the desk, a pale, hawk-featured man with thick greying hair above a high forehead . . . the formidable Sir Thomas himself, or so it must be assumed. He realised with some amusement that this unknown situation was being thrown at him to deal with; in the hope, no doubt, of discomfiting him. There was certainly no friendliness in the pale eyes that were studying him; the older man's look, so far as it could be read, was one of detached speculation. And his voice was non-committal as he went on:

"The wife of one of our employees has reported to the police that her husband is missing." He looked back to the sergeant. "Mr. Maitland has only just joined us, Murray. But all the same, as a lawyer, this seems to come within his terms of reference."

Murray, who had murmured an acknowledgment to the introduction in a comfortable, north-country voice, glanced again briefly at the newcomer, and then back at Sir Thomas. He was a big man with a hefty pair of shoulders, a blunt, freckled face, and wiry, reddish hair. He said now, with an effect of stubbornness: "It hadn't occurred to you, sir, that the company should advise us——?"

"No," said Sir Thomas. It did not seem to strike him that to amplify his statement was either desirable or necessary. Antony decided it was time he entered the discussion.

"Are you talking about Carleton?" he said.

"We are," said Murray.

"Mr. Knowles told me he'd heard from Mrs. Carleton." Antony spoke with nervous earnestness, and felt Sir Thomas's eyes upon him, consideringly. "He was sorry she was worried, of course; but there wasn't much we could do, in the circumstances."

"Well, that's what I want to understand, sir; what circumstances?"

"Such a delicate matter, Sergeant. We should have been unwilling to embarrass Mrs. Carleton."

"You think he has gone away for some domestic reason?"

"What else?" Antony had come farther into the room by this time, and stood near the corner of the desk. The move had brought Constable Gill more into his line of vision; a man taller than his superior officer, and less heavily built, with dark, sleek hair, a sallow complexion, and mild brown eyes. Perhaps because their eyes met just then, it was he who answered the query, saying quietly but with no effect of awkwardness:

"There were other things suggested . . . when we were here before."

"You mean, when young Homer was killed?" (Even a new employee might be presumed to have picked up so much gossip.) "But surely the inquest cleared all that up," he added, innocently.

"Well, did it, sir?"

Sir Thomas cleared his throat, and spoke quickly into the pause that followed the constable's query. "I had certainly supposed so," he said sharply.

Antony (partly, it must be admitted, from sheer perversity, but partly to serve his own ends) said earnestly: "Accidents *will* happen." And had the satisfaction of seeing an irritated scowl on the older man's face before Sir Thomas retreated again into his rather enigmatic silence. "I don't really see the connection," he added diffidently, with an inquiring look at the police sergeant.

"Mrs. Carleton tells me her husband worked in the Missile Division," said Murray, re-entering the conversation with apparent irrelevance.

"He does," said Sir Thomas, grimly. His tone underlined, faintly, his use of the present tense.

"And so did Mr. Homer, I believe?"

This was getting altogether too near home. "Meaning . . . what, Sergeant?"

"Meaning, sir, I don't like coincidences."

"But there's no question . . . look here, what *did* Mrs. Carleton tell you?"

"She was inclined to be hysterical."

"And talked about hush-hush jobs and atomic spies, I shouldn't wonder," said Antony. And allowed his amusement to appear.

The two policemen exchanged glances. "All the same," said Murray, with his air of quiet persistence, "we should like to talk to some of Mr. Carleton's colleagues. It seems he told his wife he was coming back to work, last Tuesday evening. And she never saw him again."

The choice of words caught Antony's attention, so that

he glanced sharply at the policeman. "I wonder, Sergeant——" His tone was diffident, almost nervous. "I wonder whether you don't know rather more than you're telling us." Murray turned to look at him, and their eyes met and locked with a sudden awareness of conflict.

"What's on your mind, Mr. Maitland?"

"I think," Antony spoke slowly, and could not have said afterwards upon what compulsion the words were uttered, "I think that the moor is wide. Plenty of dead ground there, where a man could lie hidden . . . or what was left of him."

"Now, there's a remarkable thing," said Murray blandly. "We found Carleton's body there, early this morning, not three hundred yards from the main Works' gate." He looked again at the man behind the desk. "So you see, sir——" Sir Thomas came to his feet; a man much shorter than he had appeared when he was seated, obviously shaken, but still in command of himself, if not entirely of the situation.

"I see there's nothing for it," he agreed, "you must make your inquiries." And only as an afterthought did he add grimly: "How did he die?"

"He was battered to death, you might say," the sergeant replied without emotion. "And not a doubt this time, Sir Thomas, that it was done deliberate."

CHAPTER SIX

IF THE LITTLE ROOM which the management of General Aircraft had allotted to their new Assistant Secretary seemed bleak and unwelcoming on the morning of his arrival, a week's occupation had changed all that. Antony, surveying the mountain of files, the clutter of papers which covered the wide top of his desk, reflected with little satisfaction that he need have had no doubts as to the amount of protective cover the job would afford him. When William Knowles claimed he needed an assistant, he had spoken, it seemed, no more than the truth. The company, in fact, had some octopus-like attributes, and would willingly have absorbed him completely; he found to his surprise that he did not altogether resent this, that his attitude to the task he had undertaken had changed insensibly during the past seven days.

When George and Stephen had come to him, he had diagnosed their anxiety, cynically enough, as of selfish origin; and this same preoccupation he found now in their colleagues. But there was something beyond that, too. The factory was geared to work of a certain kind, and what would happen—even to the non-classified contracts—if the Ministry lost confidence? This was something that would affect not only the men directly concerned, but all the vast complex of departments which made up the Carcroft works. From the Factory Manager, to the newest recruit in Assembly; Purchasing, and Sales, and Accounts, and Wages; the administrative staff, the transport drivers, and the members of the Corps of Commissionaires; all would, sooner or later, feel the effect of the cancellation of present contracts, and the failure to obtain new ones.

Sir Thomas, however, remained an enigma. One could not hazard the remotest guess as to his feelings. Except that—obviously—his dislike of having an outsider foisted on him had crystallised at an early date into a personal dislike for the newcomer.

Harry Carleton's body had been found near the works, and not very far from the main road. It lay in a fold of the moor, without attempt at concealment, but invisible to any incurious passer-by. Antony, however, felt it was little wonder the police search had come across it so quickly. From the medical evidence it seemed likely that death had occurred on the night of Carleton's disappearance; as for the cause, there was no doubt at all—he had been hit about the head again and again, perhaps with a heavy walking-stick or some similar weapon. Antony, listening to a description of the wounds, hoped silently that some other relative might be available to spare the widow the ordeal of identification.

The gate-house book showed that the dead man's visit to the laboratory that night had been a brief one, from eight forty-five to eight fifty-seven. Presumably he had driven away in his own car. "And that puzzles me," said Antony, talking it over in the privacy of Knowles's office. "Why should it be missing?"

"I don't know," Knowles conceded. "But no difficulty about hiding it, if you know the moor."

"No, but in that case, why leave Carleton where he must be found?"

Knowles shrugged, and spread his hands helplessly. "I haven't a notion, dear boy," he confessed. "You tell me."

Antony declined the invitation, but the question remained an irritation at the back of his mind. Sir Thomas was more interested in the men who had worked late in the laboratory that evening, and he gave him, when pressed, as much as he had been able to glean of the result of the police inquiries. "Naylor was here, and Tom Burns—who is in his section, isn't he? Burns went home before Carleton arrived. Naylor remained, and the two of them left together."

"And what," asked Sir Thomas, "has Master Stephen to say to *that*?"

"They parted on the car-park." Antony's tone was flat, and made no concession to the note of satisfaction that was audible in the other man's voice. "Naylor's car was nearer the exit. He drove off immediately, and doesn't remember whether Carleton passed him on the way to town. He rather thinks not."

Sir Thomas pursed his lips. Knowles said encouragingly: "That sounds reasonable enough." The encouragement, Antony thought, was for his own flagging spirits. The Managing Director snapped: "Reasonable!" and looked challengingly around him.

"There was only one other person in the lab that evening. Weston was in his office; he didn't see Carleton, though he actually left while he was in the lab."

"After all," said Sir Thomas, "this doesn't really get us anywhere." He spoke quickly, and frowned as he spoke.

"It all depends," Antony remarked gently, "on where we want to get." Knowles gave him a puzzled look. Sir Thomas said, angrily:

"I see nothing clever in standing about making cryptic remarks."

"Nothing whatever," agreed Antony cheerfully. "But I don't even know whether I'm interested in Carleton's death, you know."

"I should have thought it obvious———"

"The police, I believe, have stopped trying to connect his murder with the accident to Homer."

"Well, at least," said Sir Thomas with an air of triumph, "they haven't ceased to suspect Stephen Naylor."

And that, Antony reflected, reviewing the situation in his own office on the Tuesday morning of the second week he spent at Carcroft, was only too obvious. Sergeant Murray might have decided that his first ideas on motive were too imaginative to be true; but his instinct for the obvious had caused him to fasten his suspicions firmly on the one man who was known to have been in Carleton's company the evening he disappeared. "Take care of the facts and

the motive will take care of itself" might be a good slogan
(and as a lawyer, he must approve it), but on its present
line the police investigation promised to be more of a
hindrance than a help to his own researches.

He had spoken rather more frankly with Josiah Akeroyd
when at last he found himself in his office in the Technical
Block that first Monday afternoon. This was of necessity;
he needed information about the Full Moon project and the
men who were working on it which the Managing Director
was probably not able, and certainly showed no sign of
being willing to give.

Akeroyd was a tall, loose-jointed man, with fluffy white
hair and a healthy brick-coloured complexion. His accent
remained stubbornly that of a dalesman, but varied in
intensity with every change of mood. "It's a bad business," he said sombrely. "Young Homer . . . and now,
Harry Carleton."

"You think, then, that the first death was not an accident?" Antony spoke cautiously, feeling his way.

"Stephen said all along it was murder. There was some
bad feeling about that." Akeroyd paused, and looked at
his companion as though daring him to make more of his
words than the simple face value of his statement. "And
Harry was hinting at some knowledge of what had happened that night." He shook his head as though he were
puzzled. "It wouldn't have mattered what happened that
night, unless Bill's death . . . unless it was deliberate."

"What exactly did Carleton say?"

"I only got this at second-hand, you know. But I suppose I must tell you." He spoke heavily, and with obvious
distaste. "He said he had been with Sir Thomas that
evening, and left him about half past eight. His own car
was being repaired, and the M.D. offered him a lift to
town; so he went outside to wait. Well, that's all there was
to it, really; something happened, that's obvious . . . he
wouldn't say what." Josiah paused, and glared again at his
companion as though daring him to comment adversely on
his story. "What he *did* say, it had been an interesting
evening. Interesting, and instructive. That's what he *said*."

"Yes, I see." (A foggy night; something he heard,

then, rather than something seen.) "You think, perhaps, that Carleton was killed because he had some knowledge——?"

"Not my province." There was satisfaction in Akeroyds tone, and his speech broadened momentarily. "I'll tell thee owt I can, young man, owt I *know*. But I'll be damned if I'll guess."

"Well, what you know, sir . . . that would include the people in the Missile Division, wouldn't it? I can't get them sorted out," he added, plaintively.

"If that's *all*," said the older man, doubtfully, "there's a list somewhere." Though he spoke vaguely, his record-keeping was obviously precise, and he produced the list from the second drawer of his filing cabinet without any hesitation at all. "Here you are," he said. Antony took from him a double sheet of foolscap paper, which was covered with names; it seemed that the size of print and the amount of inset from the margin had some significance. Such varied descriptions as "Flight Simulation," "Environmental Testing," "Superintendent, Model Shop," blurred under his fascinated gaze. After a moment:

"That simplifies matters tremendously," he said, and looked up at his companion with an appreciative grin.

Josiah had taken pity on his ignorance after that, and without any sign of despising it, for which he was grateful. "What precisely is the trouble, lad?" he asked.

"There are too many people." Antony waved the list in a distraught way to illustrate his point. "It would take a year to sort them out, let alone——"

"Well, what I thought, you'd be looking for alibis . . . things like that."

Antony resigned himself to the tedium of explanation. "I got all that from Milner," he said. "The night of the fog was hopeless, everything disorganised . . . they couldn't turn up anything helpful at all."

"Yes, I can imagine. But——"

"The trouble is, you see, if Bill Homer really was murdered it was the work of two men. If you postulate a principal and at least one accomplice . . . well, you can see for yourself alibis cease to mean anything so far as the other incidents are concerned.''

''You mean, one might be at home in bed, while the other . . . yes, I see.''

''There is the further difficulty,'' said Antony, almost apologetically, ''that obviously there have been more incidents than we know of.'' He ignored Akeroyd's startled look, and added thoughtfully: ''I noticed a door marked 'Dark Room' when I was down in the lab to-day. I take it——''

''We have complete facilities, of course.''

''Who uses the equipment? Is there any check——?''

''Anyone who needs it. I don't think——''

''So no one would notice if—say—some microfilm were missing?''

''No . . . no. You think that's what is happening?''

''I think only that it's very likely. Naylor's letter was missing for a day . . . I understand it would have been passed on to you in the normal course, and so been no longer available. But if the photographic facilities are there for anyone to use, that doesn't help me any more than your suggestion about alibis.'' Antony sounded disconsolate.

''You're right about that,'' said Akeroyd. He looked up, and smiled grimly. ''How do you propose to get round that, young man?''

''I intend to assume that the principal, at least, has some particular knowledge of the Full Moon project. It is not necessarily a valid assumption,'' he added. ''I realise that. But I've got to make a start somewhere.''

Even then, it had taken some time to bring Akeroyd to the point, and considerable energy to keep him there. ''You don't mean particular knowledge,'' he pointed out. ''You mean, you want to know who has an overall knowledge of the project, in all its aspects.'' Antony assented, a little wearily. ''Well, I have, for one,'' said Josiah, eyeing him challengingly.

''So I suppose,'' agreed Antony, unmoved.

''Well, then!'' He held out his hand for the list, which he spread out on the desk before him, and circled the names as he spoke. ''Of the people directly concerned with Full Moon, there'd be John Lund, of course . . . he's in charge of the development. And of the people under him, Evan Williams would probably be the one with the most comprehensive knowledge; he's in charge of the U.K. Trials, so he might not have the information very early, but it would all be available to him, of course." He paused, and peered at his companion, as though doubting his ability to assimilate the information that was being laid before him. "On the Research side, the whole computer group; and Vlasov, too, partly because of his job, which is Systems Study, and partly because a good many of Weston's responsibilities seem to fall on him."

"Then should we add Weston too?"

"*If* he was capable of understanding the information at his disposal," said Josiah sourly.

"And speaking of the computer group——"

"Well?"

"The information that was said to have got out the first time—when the Ministry started making inquiries—I understood Ramsey to say it was something known only to the computer group."

"At the time, yes, in a way." His reluctance was very obvious now. "It was something they had come to know as the result of some runs they had been doing; that isn't to say it wasn't available to any of the others, you know."

"Within the limits you have outlined above, I take it?"

"They'd be the people with the most general view of the project," Josiah agreed sadly. "And I think you're 'appen right to make that assumption . . . it isn't just a matter of one man's knowledge, it's knowing what there is to know, if you see what I mean."

"I think I do."

"But that's just from your point of view. As far as I'm concerned, I just can't believe in either murder or treason . . . not among people I know."

"You've no doubt that a knowledge of Full Moon would be valuable?"

"A defensive weapon," said Akeroyd. "An anti-missile missile . . . of all ridiculous phrases. Of incalculable importance, if only we can perfect it . . . there've been

RICHARD WESTON   **?**   Chief of Research
Basil Vlasov   Systems Study
    Alec MacIntyre   do.
    Geoffrey Wood   do.
    Arthur Cockburn   do.
Stephen Naylor   Computer Group
    William Homer   do.
    Thomas Burns   do.
Roy Donaldson   Propulsive Methods
    David Green   do.
    Matthew Trench   do.
Robert Smith   Advance Projects
Henry Roberts   Guidance
    Henry Dyer   do..   *JOSIAH!*
    Joseph Tobin   do.
    Donald Lawrence   do.
Edward Ross   Auto-pilot
    Wayne Nesbit   do.
    James Neale   do.
JOHN LUND   Chief Development Engineer
John Sotheby   Flight Simulation
    William Hammond   do.
    George Sutton   do.
Henry Carleton DEC'D Hydraulics **X**
    Sidney Meynell   do.   *RAMSEY* **X** (IN LAB)
    Alfred Adamson   do.
    Thomas Gardner   do.
Richard Appleby   Manufacturing Methods **X**
    Charles Edwards   do.
Robert Mellor   Chief Draughtsman
Evan Williams   U.K. Trials
    James Trent   do.
Francis Cecil   Environmental Testi
    Ian Barrie

snags, you know; when the formula for the fuel was developed we'd practically to start again. Well, that's an exaggeration, but the modifications needed were pretty extensive.''

''How is the work coming along?''

''Well . . . very well.''

''And to get back to people: what about Dick Appleby, for instance?'' Antony spoke slowly, trying to recall as he did so the details of his talk with Stephen about the missing letter. ''Carleton himself? George Ramsey?''

''In each case, a strictly limited knowledge.''

''All right then, we'll leave it for now.'' Antony took the list of staff with him when he left, and its length continued to depress him.

Now, a week later, he was wondering a little dejectedly how much real knowledge his subsequent research had added to the results of that first interview with Josiah. Already the organisation of the firm was more familiar, he was sorting out the men he was interested in . . . but who was to say that he was giving his inquiries the right direction?

He was standing by the window of his office, which gave him a bleak enough prospect, but one which he found oddly attractive. When he heard the door open he turned, and met Mickey's accusing look. (The nickname, he had learned, was short for Carmichael; he had never heard her Christian name.)

''Are you looking for that agreement? It's here somewhere——''

''Well, I know Mr. Knowles wants it, but I don't think he *expects* it yet. I came to tell you we'd made coffee early, and as you're so busy I'm sure you can do with a cup to revive you.''

Antony laughed. ''I was thinking, Mickey; I find that very hard work.''

''Then come along.'' She started across the landing ahead of him, but stopped short as she saw a young man who was coming from one of the rooms at the back of the house. ''Hallo, Tom!'' she said. Antony recognised the young man, who was auburn-haired and freckled, as

Tom Burns who worked under Naylor in the Computer Group. Looking at him now over Mickey's shoulder, Antony was startled by his pallor. He might almost have been in a state of shock, and looked at the girl for a long moment before his eyes seemed to focus on her face. He pulled himself together with an obvious effort. "Hallo, Mickey." His smile was ghastly.

Strangely enough she did not, as might have been natural, ask if he was ill. She said: "Have some coffee, Tom."

"I don't think . . . I ought to go——" He half turned towards the stairs, but stopped abruptly as he saw Stephen coming up.

The week that had passed had left its mark on Stephen Naylor; he had a look of strain that seemed now to be permanent, but his voice was calm as he spoke. "Good lord, Tom, what are you doing over here?"

"That report for Knight. Sir Thomas wanted it. I left it with Miss Macaulay." He made an obvious effort to speak normally, looked again for a moment at Mickey, and then brushed past his colleague and disappeared down the stairs.

Stephen shrugged, and looked after him only a moment. "I wanted to see you, Antony." (Here, Christian names were in order. To the newcomer, used to a different custom among his own colleagues, it seemed strange that he should now address his old schoolfellow as "George," whereas at twelve years old he would have scorned anything less formal than "Ramsey.")

"Can it wait? I've got an invitation for coffee, and Mickey seems in a generous mood." He looked down at the girl, who was still staring after Tom Burns, and whose look was troubled. "What about it, Mickey?"

"Well, of course." It was one of William Knowles's more amiable characteristics, that his secretary could declare open house at coffee time; he had once confided to Antony that he got more information that way about what was happening in the firm, than by a dozen official meetings, but the younger man doubted whether in any case he would have been inclined to veto the proceedings.

Mickey had time to take only a couple of steps in the

direction of her office when the door leading to Sir Thomas's room burst open and Josiah Akeroyd shot out on to the landing. He turned and looked back into the Managing Director's office, and shook his fist—an unlikely gesture, but somehow, from him, believable. "I tell thee, Tom," he said impressively, "tha's gotten wrong end of t'stick." Sir Thomas's answer was audible only as a low, growling sound, and he went on impatiently: "I'm telling thee, lad, tha'll regret it," and slammed the door. Mickey was standing with her mouth open; Stephen had assumed a look of elaborate unconcern; Antony's expression was one of friendly interest; and Akeroyd, after glaring at them for a moment, remarked "Humph!" loudly; added, incomprehensibly: "I don't believe a word of it!" and stumped off down the stairs.

"What on earth was all that?" asked Susie Jenner, looking up as they trooped into her office a moment later.

"Only Josiah," said Mickey, airily.

"He was denouncing the M.D." Stephen explained. "Do you know what's biting him?"

"Well . . . not really." Susie gave him a troubled look. "They often disagree."

"Josiah doesn't often get *completely* Yorkshire," said Mickey. She had gone to the tray, but her hand shook a little as she passed Antony his cup, and she did not raise her eyes as she went on: "Nothing's been the same since Harry was killed. I sometimes wonder——"

"It isn't any use worrying." Susie gave her sudden, warm smile at the young girl, who looked back doubtfully and with unwonted gravity. "Things pass, don't they?" she appealed to the two men.

Before either of them could reply there was an interruption. Evan Williams had come through the door from the Secretary's office and, having obviously overheard something of what had been said, was prepared to make the most of it dramatically and even emotionally. "It will not pass, indeed, that Harry is dead," he remarked. "Or that somebody killed him."

"But what we really mind," said Mickey, with a return to her normal manner and a rather terrifying candour, "what we really mind is the police thinking it was one of us." Her gesture, embraced the whole works. Susie looked at her oddly, and again (as on his first morning at Carcroft) Antony had the impression of hidden, guarded knowledge.

"That is not surprising. But I do not think they ask the right questions," Evan complained. Antony stirred his coffee and asked idly:

"What would the right questions be?"

"About Stephen's letter." He added quickly, as Naylor stiffened: "And about Bill's death, and the papers of mine that were tampered with, that someone had been reading." He looked round the little group in a challenging way; but they had all heard this complaint before, and showed now very little sign of interest.

"I don't think, you know, that the police connect Carleton's death with these security problems of yours." Antony's statement had a tentative air. He was watching Williams, whose face reflected so many emotions, so rapidly, as to be almost completely unreadable; but a movement of Mickey's caught his attention, so that he glanced round at her quickly and caught, for a moment, a stricken look in her eyes. Evan said:

"Then they should do!" positively; and she relaxed again, with a look that was very like relief, and gave her attention to her coffee-making. "And as for Bill getting killed like that——"

"We thought at the time it was an accident," said Susie. "But Bill and then Harry, so soon——"

"They don't need to look so far for a motive in the case of a chap like Carleton," said Stephen. Unexpectedly, this remark seemed to upset the Welshman; he put down his half-empty cup with deliberation. "Indeed to goodness, Stephen Naylor, that is not a nice thing to say." The other man's look of incomprehension only seemed to infuriate him further. He gave an angry exclamation, and marched out of the room.

Stephen's bewilderment seemed genuine enough. "What on earth was all that about——?"

"Oh, Stephen, really!" Susie was half laughing, half exasperated. "You know how touchy he is."

"But what did I say?"

"He was in love with Linda when she worked for Mr. Daly, before she married Harry. You must have known that, Stephen."

"Well, I suppose so. What of it?"

"No one could say Harry was exactly a success as a husband, and I don't suppose that endeared him to Evan," said Susie, with admirable understatement.

"Oh, lord, I didn't mean——" Stephen sounded genuinely contrite. Susie did not reply to that, but turned her eyes towards the younger girl for a moment. Mickey had gone back to her own desk and was reading—or seeming to read—something from her shorthand notebook; the flush showed painfully against the clear pallor of her skin, but she did not look up or make any other sign that she was attending to what went on. A rather awkward silence lengthened. Antony, who was intrigued by the situation but saw no profit in probing it, as it were, in open court, drank the last of his coffee and put the cup down on the tray.

"Finished, Stephen?" he inquired; and receiving a nod from the other man, made for the door. "I'll try and have that draft licence agreement ready for you after lunch," he added, to Susie. "But I've got to see somebody about the technical terms—they sound most unlikely!"

She smiled at that. "They always do. But it gives the engineers something to despise us about, which is probably good for their self-esteem."

"I can't say most of us need much encouragement," said Stephen. He spoke absently; his attention was fixed on Susie, who looked at him now and said deliberately:

"I don't think I agree with you." But she seemed to have forgotten the subject almost before the two men were out of the room. As he closed the door Antony heard her say: "Mickey, are you all right?" And there was an urgency in her voice that he had not heard before.

Back in Antony's office, Stephen seemed to find some difficulty in coming to the point. He stood by the window, and drummed his fingers on the glass, and said without looking round: "Evan's a queer chap, temperamental. I didn't mean to upset him."

"I don't suppose," said Antony, seating himself behind the desk, "I don't suppose for a moment she thought you did." He grinned as he saw the other man's shoulders stiffen, but his expression was sober enough by the time Stephen turned to look at him.

"Susie?" he asked, gloomily. "Well, perhaps she didn't, but she took me up quickly enough. However——"

"You wanted to talk to me," Antony reminded him.

"Yes, I . . . you know, I meant to ask Evan, if only he hadn't flown off the handle like that. That business of the estimates——"

"If you mean," said Antony, glancing down at a letter on his desk to refresh his memory, "that the estimates are likely to be greatly exceeded due to the fact that a tactical requirement has arisen for launching from shipboard; and that consequently the full-scale simulation of these conditions is necessary—" (Stephen was gaping at him.) "That's all been settled."

"But it can't have been," Naylor protested. "They'll have to make a platform . . . a large platform . . . capable of rotation on its own axis. And the required load-carrying capacity . . . well, I know it can be done, but have you thought what the Ministry are likely to say about the additional cost?"

"Don't worry, dear boy," said Antony, with a fair imitation of William Knowles's manner. "I spent the whole of yesterday morning drafting that letter—which is why I'm so word-perfect—but now it isn't needed. Evan and the Flight Simulation chap got Willie all worked up, but when he managed to get hold of Lund he came up with the answer. I can only imagine he must find continued association with Evan stimulates the intellect."

"You still haven't told me——"

"Oh, Lund happened to remember they're breaking up the *King George V*. So all we have to do is get on to the Admiralty and ask for one of her turrets." He shifted the papers on his desk. "This is the new letter," he said. "We ask for one of her turrets, and mount our roll and pitch hydraulics on it. I say, I think I've missed my real vocation, don't you? At least, I'm learning the language.''

Stephen laughed. "Well, we can but try." He paused, and his companion guessed, accurately enough, that they were nearing the real point of the meeting. "I've just had another session with the police.''

Antony leaned back, and gestured towards the one spare chair the office boasted. "Unpleasant?'' he queried.

"I found it so." Stephen took the offered chair and leaned forward with his arms on the desk. "I don't understand what they think. I mean, they don't seem to be connecting Harry's death with what went before——''

"They are concentrating, very properly, on opportunity.''

"But I had no reason——'' His voice rose on the protest.

"Then you may be thankful. They won't move without one, on the evidence they've got. Murray's too wise a bird for that.''

"There must be a connection, though. And if they come back to that theory——''

"If I were you,'' said Antony flatly, "I wouldn't cross that bridge until you get to it.''

"No, but . . . well, I was wondering . . . I know a week isn't long, but have you any idea——?''

"Good lord, a hundred!'' He moved restlessly, uncomfortably aware of the constriction of movement that the tiny room imposed. "Tell me about Tom Burns, Stephen; what's up with him?''

Naylor's lips tightened. Obviously he did not like the query, but it was characteristic of the attitude he had adopted towards the inquiry that he gave it consideration and answered as well as he could. "He was upset by Bill's death. And there's been talk, it hasn't been pleasant for either of us.''

"If he has any guilty knowledge——''

"I don't believe it!'' Stephen spoke impulsively. "I've done my best not to intrude my own opinions on you, Antony, but he's a good lad.''

"Well balanced?''

"Are any of us? He's—well, he's an idealist I grant you. Takes a lot of living up to."

"I don't much like the sound of that," said Antony soberly. And added, with a burst of irritation: "And don't ask me what I mean, because I'm damned if I know myself."

"I suppose," said the other slowly, "you mean if *they* were both traitors . . . oh, lord, how unlikely that sounds!"

"Go on." Maitland's tone was unsympathetic. "You'll get nowhere by being afraid of words."

"Well then: if they *were*, and Tom knew it——"

"That was in my mind, certainly. If it comforts you at all, however, I can't help but feel that Homer and Carleton make an unlikely pair of conspirators."

"Yes!" said Stephen with feeling. He got to his feet, and looked down at his companion with a rueful smile. "I'm sorry, I'm wasting your time. I used to think I wasn't easily rattled."

"This binge you're having in the lab," said Antony, ignoring this threat of self-abasement. "What about it?"

"Christmas Eve? Well, we always have a few drinks, and though none of us feel specially festive this year, the idea seems to be we should proceed as usual."

"Will you be there?"

"I don't see any prospect of getting out of it. Why?"

Antony did not answer directly. "Weston invited me," he said. "I was wondering why."

"He's George's brother-in-law," said Naylor, unhelpfully. Antony cocked an amused eye at him.

"Friend of yours?" he inquired.

"I've nothing against him," said Stephen; but added with a burst of candour: "He's a damned smooth-spoken fellow, and no good at his job!"

"Well, be that as it may," said Antony, "I accepted his invitation. Gratefully," he added; and grinned at Stephen's look of disgust.

CHAPTER SEVEN

BY LUNCH-TIME the fact that Chief Engineer and Managing Director had once again been in conflict was pretty common knowledge. Antony, sharing a table with George, John Lund and Basil Vlasov, was entertained by the imaginative variety of the speculations he heard on all sides. Catching Lund's eye, he became aware of a sardonic look. "You don't believe," he inquired, "that Sir Thomas *is* interfering with the technical specifications."

Lund smiled back at him, but answered seriously enough. "Anything else," he said. "Not that." Basil, who had been chewing his way dreamily through a plateful of rather grey-looking beef, came to life at that and said with his deceptive air of solemnity:

"Nor even that our Josiah is entertaining a guilty passion for Miss Macaulay?"

George's laugh, in anyone less dignified, could only have been called a snigger. Antony said: "I hadn't heard that one." And Lund remarked with a grin:

"You invented it, Basil. Don't tell me!"

"Oh, no, I didn't." He looked around at his audience with an air of triumph. "I have no imagination, you know," he added. "I couldn't have thought of anything so perfect."

"I expect," said George, whose attention seemed to have wandered, "that it was about Weston again." He ignored Lund's look of irritation and explained to Antony: "Richard was Sir Thomas's appointment, and Akeroyd never approved."

"What was his objection?"

"Technical," said Lund quickly. "Purely technical." As

this statement seemed calculated to add to the general obscurity, Antony probed gently.

"How long ago was that?"

"He came to the lab four or five years ago. It's nearly two years now since Lemming retired, and he got the appointment."

"Over my head," said Basil, helping himself absent-mindedly to more potatoes. He seemed to speak without malice; and, strangely, his words did not appear to add to Lund's embarrassment. The Chief Development Engineer relaxed a little, saying:

"Well, we all know you do the work, Basil. But you can't say it adds to the general efficiency of Research." He began to look about him, trying to attract the attention of the hearty local girl who acted as waitress. Antony finished his beef, and listened idly to a rather one-sided argument that had developed between George and Basil, as to which of them suffered the more from Weston's deficiencies. Looking about him, he saw that the Chief of Research was not lunching in the canteen that day. Lund, seeing his look, said abruptly:

"He's gone to London. The trip Harry should have made two weeks ago."

George interrupted himself to greet this information with an incredulous exclamation. "Surely someone from your department——" He laid down his knife and fork, and seemed prepared to hold an inquisition into the matter. "I don't think Weston knew anything about hydraulics," he added.

"He doesn't," said Lund, who seemed to find the subject distasteful.

"He's gone on *our* affairs," said Basil. "One of Bob Smith's bright ideas. The hydraulics report is incidental."

"I see." George sounded portentous, as though the enterprise should somehow have had his sanction, but perhaps might be considered not altogether ill-advised. "He'll be back before Christmas, I suppose."

"He will!" said Lund. He did not sound enthralled by the prospect, and George looked positively downcast. With the obvious intention of changing the subject he asked presently:

"Can't you do anything about Evan, John?"

Lund was prodding a portion of apple-pie with a cautious fork. "What has Evan been doing?" he asked calmly.

"Well, ever since someone disarranged his papers, he's been absolutely dotty on security."

"I'm glad to hear it."

"Yes, but . . . dammit, John, nothing gets done. I wanted him to anticipate his report on the performance of the modified tail-ring assembly, but if you knew the act he puts on about answering a simple question——"

"Very proper," said Lund, with a faint smile twisting the corners of his mouth. "Think how pleased the Ministry would be."

"They won't be pleased if they don't get the hardware," said George flatly.

"I suppose not. But you'll just have to put up with it, George. There's no doing anything with Evan once he's made his mind up. Not that I believe for a moment that anyone really interfered with his papers," he added, reflectively. "His things are always in such a muddle——"

"Oh, but that's where you're wrong!" Basil looked up from his pudding with his lazy smile. "Easy enough to put things back as you found them if they were tidy to begin with; and haven't you noticed how these chaps who look as if they're working in the ruins of a bomb explosion always manage to produce what you want at a moment's notice?"

"Well, so can you," George pointed out.

"Yes, but if someone searched my desk and took care about it, I doubt if I'd ever know."

"I'll take your word for it." George sounded doubtful.

"Anyway, the important thing about Evan at the moment is his pet theory about the things that have been happening. He's decided," said Basil, looking round to make sure that he had his companion's attention, "he's decided that I'm a Communist."

George greeted this with a shout of laughter, and even Lund, who had shown signs of uneasiness ever since the conversation originally turned towards Richard Weston, smiled with unaffected amusement. Antony said vaguely:

"I suppose to anyone as—as mercurial as Evan——"

"He hasn't said so, of course," Basil interrupted, "but he's taken to haunting me; I suppose he thinks he's being unobtrusive, but I'm beginning to get rattled." (It was only too obvious that this statement had no basis in fact.) "When are his next lot of trials coming off, John?"

Lund shrugged. "Ask the meteorologists. Not for some time, unless we get some clearer days." He pushed away his plate, and looked from his colleagues to the new Assistant Secretary. "Richard tells me you're joining us on Christmas Eve, Antony. Does that mean you're staying at Holly Royd over the holiday? I'm afraid your wife will be finding it dull."

"Yes, we're staying. But you don't know Jenny, she's never bored."

"She's house hunting, perhaps?" Lund's tone was idle. George said, a little too quickly:

"Beryl's been showing her round." And Antony added, concealing his irritation well enough:

"We aren't in too much of a hurry. Mrs. Ambler makes us very comfortable, and she's teaching Jenny to make parkin at the moment——"

"Well, I'm sorry I'm not in a position to do any entertaining. Mrs. Foster's a good soul but not really up to coping with guests." Lund got up as he spoke, and went on without giving them time for comment, "I don't think I'll wait for coffee."

Antony murmured something. He watched Lund threading his way between the tables, and turned to find Basil's eyes fixed on him inquiringly. Just for a moment he was looking, not sleepy, but coldly intelligent; but his voice when he spoke was gentle as ever. "John's wife died two years back," he said. "He took it hard."

"Too hard," said George. And seemed taken aback by his own candour. "Well, you know, I mean——"

"For once in your life, exactly what you say." Basil's smile robbed the words of offence. "Grief is one thing—"

he added. And stirred his coffee; and did not see—or at any rate ignored—Antony's look of inquiry.

Later that afternoon, he was looking for Josiah Akeroyd, and ran him to earth at last in the Air Frame Assembly Shed with George in harassed attendance. "What do you think of 'Full Moon,' Maitland?" he asked, waving a proprietorial hand.

Antony looked about him: sleek, highly polished monsters they seemed, with their slaves in servile attendance; but surprisingly unimpressive as they lay about in various stages of completion. "Jolly little things, aren't they?" he said vaguely. "Just like the films," he added. George gave a snort of disgust at this inept comment, and went away muttering about "fin ring assembly." The Chief Engineer grinned at his companion, and shook his head at him.

"Well, you know," said Maitland, "this one, for instance, looks finished. So why isn't its nose sharp?"

"Not until it's armed," said Josiah. He gave it a friendly pat, and turned on the other man a look that was suddenly penetrating. "And what do you think of *us*?" he asked.

"It's a very interesting experience," said Antony cautiously. "I've a lot to learn, I'm afraid." The other grinned appreciatively.

"Don't be so damned demure," he said. "Nobody'll hear us, with all this row going on. I've been wanting to talk to you again." He turned away as he spoke, and Antony fell into step beside him, but made no attempt to reply until they halted again near the passage-way that led to the old house. "Well?" said Josiah.

"Nothing to report," said Antony, and met his eye squarely. Akeroyd looked suddenly anxious.

"Not young Stephen?" he asked.

"Have you any reason to think so?"

"Only the M.D. A damned, pig-headed feller. But Stephen isn't a chap to explain himself: take me or leave me attitude, and I don't know that I blame him."

Maitland did not reply immediately. "I'd give a good

deal," he said at last, slowly, "to understand Sir Thomas's attitude."

"Never liked the lad; no idea of ingratiating himself. But the technical appointments are my affair, after all."

"But not Weston's appointment?"

"No!" Josiah's mouth closed on the word like a rattrap. His pale blue eyes were suddenly cold with anger. "He has the last word, of course, when he wants it."

"I see. Weston is, perhaps, a friend of his," Antony hazarded.

"Nothing of the sort. Dislikes the feller, I should say. Just his obstinacy." He stopped short, and looked at his companion doubtfully. "Just his obstinacy," he repeated. Antony grinned at him.

"As a matter of interest, sir, was that the cause of your disagreement with Sir Thomas this morning?"

"The subject was touched on." Akeroyd seemed to have recovered his good humour. "There was also the question of your appointment, Maitland," he added blandly.

"Not my worry, I'm glad to say," said Antony. "But surely you're not expecting results already?"

"I think he felt that something in the nature of an interim report——"

"Out of the question," said Antony, but did not offer to elaborate.

"Well, and so I thought, lad." For the first time since the conversation started, Akeroyd's speech broadened. He broke off as one of the doors from the works swung open and Dick Appleby came through; Antony smiled at the Chief Engineer, and moved away down the passage, and the newcomer fell into step beside him.

"The old boy seems to have cooled off now," he remarked, as soon as they were fairly out of earshot.

"I should imagine," said Antony, "that his temper is generally of the easy come, easy go variety."

"That's true enough. All the same——" Appleby paused by the baize-covered door that led into the house, and favoured his companion with a conspiratorial look, "——he can be nasty, so I'd watch my step if you have much to do with him."

"I'll bear it in mind." Antony had returned to the gently diffident manner he had assumed since he first arrived at Holly Royd. Dick nodded to him in a condescending way, and disappeared through a door on the left of the hall, which led to the Sales Department. Ambler came from behind his reception counter, ready (as usual) for conversation. Maitland paused, and said on an impulse, interrupting the gentle flow of talk: "Has Mr. Appleby been here long?"

"Three years, just about, Mr. Maitland."

"And living at Holly Royd all the time?"

"All the time, that's why I remember so clearly. It was just after we'd papered the back room, and the missus did wonder if we should put the price up; but then she said he seemed a nice lad, and so——" He pulled himself up on the brink of indiscretion, met Antony's eye, and smiled apologetically. "Well, Mr. Maitland, sir, I reckon nowt to a lad being hard up; but nothing of that now, doing well here, I should say." Antony went upstairs a few minutes later in a thoughtful frame of mind.

"He earns £1,100 a year," he told Jenny, when they were alone in their room that evening after supper. "Would you say that was enough for the way he dresses?"

Jenny looked anxious. "He goes to Harrogate quite often," she said. "Mrs. Ambler obviously thinks The Worst; but whatever he does there, it'll cost him something. Of course, he's a bachelor, with no household expenses."

"He was hard up when he arrived, so that doesn't look like a wealthy family. That being so, his suits are of a number and quality quite unsuited to his means," said Antony, didactically. "As for his gold cigarette case——" He stretched his legs to the fire, and looked up at his wife with affectionate mockery. "Sit down, love, and don't trouble your head about it. I don't see Dick Appleby as a master mind, do you?"

"No, but . . . you don't like him much, do you?"

"Not much," said Antony, and looked down at the flames, so that Jenny could no longer see his expression. "But he isn't the only person I find interesting," he said.

"Tell me, then." She sat down, and assumed a look of expectation.

"Well, sticking to the financial angle . . . what about Basil? He's better paid than Dick, doesn't run a car. I wouldn't think he had a parsimonious nature, but he gives the impression of being hard up."

"I don't see that at all," said Jenny. "Having too much money might be suspicious, but——"

"Anything out of the ordinary." Antony spoke absently, his mind suddenly occupied with possibilities. "I admit I don't quite see——"

"There are a thousand things he might be doing with it," said Jenny. "Do you really think——?"

Hearing the troubled tone in her voice her husband smiled at her reassuringly.

"No more than I think . . . something similar . . . about half a dozen of his colleagues."

"Well . . . who?"

"Oh, good lord! There's Sir Thomas, to begin with: why does he insist on employing Weston, whom he dislikes, and whom the Chief Engineer considers incompetent? There's Josiah himself; George calls him 'eccentric,' he's certainly unselfconscious, and that's a rare enough trait, I suppose; Appleby says you have to watch your step with him. There's John Lund (keeping to the top brass); he has a habit of asking awkward questions, which may very well be fortuitous. And Richard Weston; he's a queer chap, Jenny, and I've got a feeling he's dangerous."

"Beryl doesn't like him," said Jenny, unexpectedly. (Beryl was George Ramsey's wife.) "She's said several times she can't think what Ella sees in him."

"Ella?"

"His wife, George's sister." (Antony groaned.) "Beryl likes *her*, luckily, but she hasn't any time for Richard."

"And neither has George. In fact, a more generally unpopular chap it would be hard to find."

"What are you thinking, Antony?"

"That they all take his incompetence for granted, but it might very well be a blind."

"Could he be the . . . the person you're looking for?"

Antony laughed. ''Of course he could! In common with about fifty other people. I'm guessing, love, and that's not going to get me anywhere.''

''No,'' said Jenny. ''I suppose it isn't.'' It was unlikely, of course, but an uninformed listener might almost have thought she sounded relieved.

CHAPTER EIGHT

SUSIE JENNER and Mickey had left the office at noon on Christmas Eve, so Antony felt there could be no great objection to his leaving his own office soon after three o'clock and making his way down to the Missile Division laboratory. "Though on the whole," he said to Basil, who had called him over to the 'bar,' set up incongruously on one of the benches, "you all look as if you could have done quite well without this particular manifestation of the Christmas spirit."

Basil followed his look, and smiled gently. The big room seemed full of smoke and chatter, but nobody looked particularly cheerful. "You'll feel better when you've had a drink," he said, hospitably. "What will you have? It's quite safe, you know, this isn't a chemical laboratory."

"I have learned that much," said Antony, with dignity, accepting a glass. "What do the chemists do, anyway . . . toast each other in strychnine?"

"They play it safe and come over here," said Basil. He turned to accost a small, round man whose light-coloured suit was noticeably ill-fitting, even in a company not noted for its attention to details of dress. "This is Jim Fergusson, Antony. A refugee, poor chap."

Fergusson had obviously heard something of their previous conversation. "We come over here in the kindness of our hearts," he confided. "Slumming, you might call it. We can visit them, but they can't come to us, you know." He turned back to Basil and added jovially, "How are the mods. coming along? You're certainly taking your time about them. And we told you just what was needed."

"You mustn't hurry us," said Basil. He picked up his

glass and began to move away from them with his sweet, absent smile. "This year . . . next year——" he remarked as he went. Fergusson shrugged, and moved off in his turn to join a group of his own colleagues farther down the big room. Antony refilled his glass and strolled over to where Evan Williams, excitable as ever, was haranguing Dick Appleby and three men whose faces were only vaguely familiar on the benefits of home ownership.

"But what's all this in aid of, Evan?" asked Richard Weston, coming up to them when the other man was in full flight of eloquence. "I thought your Mrs. Ryder made you pretty comfortable."

"And so she does. But there are other considerations. For a married man, now——"

"That makes a difference, of course. Are you thinking of taking a wife?" Weston was obviously deliberately misunderstanding, and his tone did not attempt to hide the malice that lay behind the question. Williams shot a look at him that was full of angry dislike.

Dick Appleby laughed. "Well, there's Antony here, house hunting," he said. "You'd better give him those figures of yours, Evan." The Welshman made a noise in his throat that was very like a growl, glared—rather unfairly—at each member of his audience in turn, drained his glass, and stumped away in the direction of the bar. Weston turned to Antony with his usual affable air.

"I'm glad to see you were able to join us. So very pleasant to be resting from our labours, and with a long week-end in prospect. I do trust that you and Mrs. Maitland will manage to be tolerably well amused." Antony, generally in sympathy with an individualist, was surprised to find himself irritated by the other man's affectations.

"Oh, I think so," he replied; and had to take deliberate thought in order to achieve the casual tone he desired. "Holly Royd isn't exactly dull, you know; and we shall be going round to the Ramseys' on Boxing Day."

"Then we shall meet there." The enthusiasm in Weston's voice made his companion sharply uncomfortable. "I shall look forward to making Mrs. Maitland's acquaintance." He glanced round, and saw his brother-in-law a few paces away, talking to John Lund. "Ah, there you are, old man. I was telling Maitland we shall be meeting on Boxing Day."

There could be little doubt, thought Antony watching the two men, that Ramsey had little relish for Weston's rather condescending affability. He smiled uneasily, and muttered something about looking forward to the occasion; this was so obviously a lie that again Antony was puzzled. This was more than dislike . . . something much more like fear, if the idea weren't so obviously ridiculous.

"Ella said she'd come over early," said Weston, apparently unaffected by any strain in the atmosphere. "Will that be all right with Beryl? I thought I'd take a gun out in the afternoon," he went on, taking the other man's consent for granted. "I'm pretty short of exercise. Will any of you join me?"

George shook his head, and felt perhaps that the gesture had been too vehement. "Too much fog about," he said apologetically. "Never knew such weather."

"Well, I shan't go far afield. Braithwaite tells me I might get a hare on his land."

"It'll be damned muddy," said George, "down by the river." His voice was hoarse, and he spoke with a degree of stubbornness that seemed unnecessary. Weston shrugged and turned to Lund, who so far had taken no part in the conversation.

"What about you, John? Don't tell me *you're* afraid of a bit of mud."

Lund smiled. "I'm going to disappoint you, all the same," he said. "While Johnny's on holiday——"

"Bring him along."

"Well, not that day. We're going to the pantomime, in Leeds."

"And Dick, I suppose, will be off to Harrogate. I hope you've got something good to take with you." His tone was light, but Appleby did not seem to relish the remark, if his frown was anything to judge by. "A Christmas present," said Weston. "Surely you aren't going to disappoint her."

Appleby smiled, and did not look amused. Lund came

to his rescue, saying smoothly: "That's always a head-ache, Christmas presents."

"Not so bad for the kids," said George; and he, too, spoke as though welcoming a change of subject. "But I suppose Johnny's getting too old for toys."

"Good heavens, yes. He's fifteen." He smiled, sud-denly, as though at some unspoken thought.

"But not too grown up for the pantomime," said Antony, idly. And saw, with surprise, that the remark was not well received. The smile lingered on Lund's face, but his eyes did not look amused.

"Well, I'm sorry you won't join me," said Weston. "We must get together before the week-end's out." He looked round as he spoke, from one of his companions to the others. The words were uttered lightly, but they were not intended, Antony realised, to be as casual as they sounded. He turned a little, and saw George's expression . . . more than dislike, certainly. Was hate too strong a word? He said quickly, from an instinctive feeling that no man's thoughts should be so openly displayed:

"Talking of presents, I suppose I should have done my shopping in Harrogate. I was trying to get my uncle a cigarette case, but there didn't seem to be much choice here." He was looking at Weston as he spoke; but it did not escape his notice that Dick Appleby, who had been taking a cigarette, snapped his case shut and slipped it back into his pocket again. There was, in fact, a rather odd little silence, before Weston said smoothly:

"Certainly you should have gone to Harrogate. Get anything you want there . . . can't you, Dick?"

"Pretty well," said Appleby. He paused a moment, and then added unnecessarily. "If you mean my cigarette case, it was a present."

"An un-birthday present," said Basil, appearing sud-denly at his elbow. Appleby frowned at him, and he added blandly: "There are, of course, many suitable occasions for an exchange of gifts."

"Sentimental occasions . . . celebrations——" Weston might have been smoothing over an awkward moment, or he might have been deliberately stirring the pot. Antony suspected the latter, but Dick laughed, quite easily now, and said:

"That was it, of course. A sentimental occasion." He moved away as he spoke; and as he did so John Lund and George Ramsey strolled together in the opposite direction. The move was so smoothly made it might have been concerted; the same urge was probably driving them both, to get away from an uncomfortable situation.

Antony looked after them, and said idly: "Lund seems very wrapped up in that boy of his." He became conscious of an alertness about Weston, and added in the same tone, "I suppose since his wife died——"

"He always thought," said Basil, "that the sun rose and set by Johnny." His words might have been an answer to Maitland's, but he was looking at Weston as he spoke.

"But still," said Richard Weston, "the shock of Margaret's death could well account for it."

"She'd been ill for a long time."

"But we all thought she was getting better." He seemed unable to leave the subject, but at the same time Antony had a strong feeling that he found it distasteful. Basil said suddenly—and this, perhaps, had been in his mind for some time, which would account for his rather desultory part in the recent conversation:

"You see a lot of George, Richard. How do you think he is?"

The question seemed to puzzle the other man. "Why . . . well. If you mean his health." He spoke uncertainly, but added more positively a moment later, "Nothing wrong with George."

Basil shrugged. "Well, you should know," he said. His smile had all its customary vagueness when he left them a few moments later.

"I'm afraid," said Weston, "that our little gathering is not quite so . . . so friendly as usual." The statement was, at best, an uncomfortable one, and did not seem to be made in any spirit of apology. Rather, Weston's look remained alert and questioning, in a way Antony was beginning to associate with him. He said vaguely:

"In the circumstances——" and allowed the sentence

to trail; there didn't really seem to be any way of finishing it.

Surprisingly, Weston laughed. "It's a grim thought," he said, and looked about him in a deliberate way, from one group of men to another. "It's the uncertainty, you know . . . suspecting each other. You're an onlooker, Maitland; what do you suppose the police are making of it all?"

"It would be interesting to know," said Antony, thoughtfully. Strangely, his companion seemed in no way irritated by his rather inadequate response.

"As a professional problem, now . . . you're a lawyer, aren't you? If you had to defend . . . well, Stephen, say." Antony followed his look across the big room: Naylor was standing near, but somehow a little aloof from, a group of his colleagues. "Never a very sociable chap," said Weston, reflectively, "but at the moment it is perhaps unwise——"

"He isn't the only one who seems to be feeling unsociable," said Antony deliberately; and as he spoke Tom Burns, who had been standing alone, walked purposefully across the room. He seemed about to speak to Stephen, but thought better of the idea and attached himself—equally silent—to the same group of men.

"To get back to Stephen," prompted Richard Weston.

"I should have to know first of all . . . on what charge?" said Antony. His tone was light and he managed to sound amused.

"Why . . . murder," said Weston. "For killing Harry Carleton, if we must be precise."

"Well, I'm afraid," said Antony apologetically, "I should say just whatever his solicitor told me to say, you know." He was looking straight at Weston as he spoke, and caught for the first time the sign of some deeper feeling than the rather malicious air of amusement that was his customary pose. "But do you think, if it came to a charge, it would be Stephen who needed defending? There's always the question of motive. I don't know any of you well enough to know about that."

"It's an interesting speculation, and depends, I suppose,

on a number of factors at present unknown to us. There's
Evan now . . . if you're interested in motives." He laughed
again at the blank look his companion gave him, and
began to move away. Antony, watching him, remembered
his own words to Jenny, and began to feel he might be
getting somewhere. But there was still—as when was there
not?—the little question of proof.

Christmas at Holly Royd was uneventful, and if Jenny
privately thought Mrs. Ambler's preoccupation with food a
little excessive, she co-operated willingly enough; though
with a strong feeling that she was taking part in provision-
ing an army.

Meanwhile, Antony relaxed. After the holiday there
would be things that could be done, but while the works
were closed there was no action he, or anybody else could
take. But that was where he was wrong.

Boxing Day was cloudy, but in spite of this Jenny
decided it was time she saw something of the countryside.
They took the car and went—inevitably—farther than they
intended, so that it was past five o'clock when they got
home, and already dark. Antony had his latch-key in the
door when he heard somebody coming up the drive, and
turned to see George Ramsey emerge from the shadows
into the narrow circle of light. His first thought was that he
had mistaken the time of the invitation, and that George
had come to seek them out. Then he saw his friend's face,
and the holiday mood left him as if it had never been.

"It's Richard . . . down by the river." George was
unconscious of Jenny's presence, unconscious of anything
but the need to unburden himself of his news. "Ella got
worried, so I went to look. He must have stumbled getting
over a stile . . . he's blown half his head off with the
shotgun."

CHAPTER NINE

THE CAPACITY of the human race for attending to business-as-usual in the face of calamity has often been remarked on; but except for their physical presence at the plant, except that they actually came to work, the employees of General Aircraft Limited displayed none of this admirable quality when the firm opened again after the long Christmas week-end. In the works there was perhaps less opportunity for uninterrupted discourse (a fact which any Production Manager will hotly deny); but the administrative workers, from the senior executives down to the boys who were putting in time in "Mailing" until they were old enough to enter the Apprentice School, were making the most of an unprecedented opportunity for gossip. Besides, there was an intriguing rumour (so far unverified) that half the Missile Division had died in agony during the holiday, presumably of slow poison. Another theory had it that Sir Thomas Overbury had been arrested; but this was generally considered unlikely, and put down to wishful thinking. Only in the laboratory itself was a certain constraint noticeable, and even there, after the first awkwardness, the volume of talk was phenomenal.

From his brief knowledge of industry, Antony Maitland could have made a fair guess at all this, but as it happened he was not in a position to observe it for himself. He had called by appointment at the Police Station in Mardingley, and was seated on a rather hard chair in Sergeant Murray's office. The sergeant, and Constable Gill who was also in attendance, had greeted him with a show of warmth; but Murray's manner was wary as he approached the point of the meeting.

"Well, now, Mr. Maitland, I'm given to understand by Sir Thomas that you're here representing the firm. But he didn't say what you wanted of us."

Antony crossed one leg over the other, and gave the policeman a deprecating look. "A delicate matter, Sergeant. You'll appreciate . . . the circumstances are unusual."

"I think we appreciate that." He glanced at his subordinate as he spoke, and Antony, following the look, thought he saw a flicker of amusement on Gill's would-be impassive face. He grinned sympathetically.

"Yes, well . . . nothing like stating the obvious. What I'm trying to say: we've no right, obviously, to ask you your business. But because the work we are doing is important—not just to the firm, but to the country as a whole—we feel that perhaps it would not be proper to ask for a certain measure of frankness."

Murray was eyeing him, his head a little on one side, a smile that seemed to be an appreciative one on his lips. Constable Gill said in his deep voice: "It would be inconvenient, I expect, if we were to arrest one of your key men without warning?"

"Exactly," said Antony. And forebore to elaborate the point. Murray said suddenly:

"You spoke of 'frankness,' Mr. Maitland. I'll be glad to co-operate." The last word was stressed, and Antony's eyebrows went up.

"I've told you all I know, Sergeant."

"That's not quite what I meant. I'll be plain with you, sir: here we have three dead men, all members of the same firm, engaged on the same project, a classified one, as I understand it. The first death could well have been an accident, but it was at that time we got a suggestion of——" He paused for a word, and Gill supplied "subversive activities," his voice more sepulchral than ever on the clumsy phrase. Murray considered this offering, nodded his approval, and went on: "Yes, well, then we have your arrival, Mr. Maitland. Your name is not unknown to me, though I didn't make the connection when first I met you."

"I've appeared, perhaps, in some case you were interested in?'' Antony's tone was politely indifferent. Murray said more brusquely:

"Very likely. But I meant that I have heard of your war record, Mr. Maitland; and of certain of your activities since then." He saw the other man compress his lips, and added, perhaps with intent to console: "Sheer bad luck from your point of view. Inspector Sykes is a good friend of mine; he was in the West Riding Constabulary before he was transferred to Central."

"And that," Antony pointed out gently, "illustrates perfectly why I do *not* wish to be frank with you."

"Yes, I see that." Murray leaned forward eagerly. "The essence of police work is common effort, the very reverse of your training. But we can help you, you know; I ask nothing in return, except just so much information as you feel free to give me."

Antony smiled at him. "And no awkward questions?" he asked. "That sounds too good to be true. All right, Murray; if you're willing to trust me, I'll keep my part of the bargain as well as I can."

The sergeant leaned back. His sigh could only have been one of relief. "Well, I don't mind telling you it's a bit beyond the normal run of things, what's been happening. And I've heard you've something of a reputation——"

"If that were true, I'd be likely to lose it over this affair." He looked from Murray to Gill, and back again to the sergeant, a look half humorous, half rueful. "Do you realise that on Christmas Eve I thought I'd finished my job . . . I was sure Weston was responsible for the leakage that had been worrying the company."

"Are you so certain now that he wasn't concerned?"

"It seems unlikely. At least, I don't think he was the principal in the affair. You've been asking questions since Boxing Day, Sergeant: do you think his death was an accident?"

"I'm bound to say it has every appearance of one." Murray was picking his words. "He'd no business to be carrying a loaded gun . . . but people do these things. His boots were muddy, of course, and there was mud on the stile; a smear of mud, as though he'd slipped. If it weren't for the other circumstances——"

"Homer's death looked like an accident, too."

"Yes," said Murray; and sighed. Gill, who—perhaps strangely—seemed less out of his depth than his colleague, asked with the directness Antony was coming to expect:

"Would you agree that Weston was not a popular man?"

"I would. In fact, I could make a guess at a number of personal reasons for wanting him out of the way. Sir Thomas was responsible for his appointment, but is said to dislike him—there's a puzzle for you! Akeroyd says he was technically incompetent, but his influence was insufficient to remove him. At least two of his subordinates in the Research Department seem to have had hopes of the job he was given; Vlasov is one of them. In general, I can't think of anybody with a good word to say for Weston——"

"And in particular," Gill put in, "there seems to have been no love lost between Mr. Ramsey and his brother-in-law."

"No, I think that's true enough." He paused and the thought persisted uncomfortably for a moment, of a sudden unexplained, uncharacteristic venom in George's look. But then . . . "but then, it seems unlikely that Weston's death was a—a domestic matter, unrelated to the others."

"Very likely."

"So we're back to the question, who could have shot him? Do you know?"

Murray shrugged. "Anybody who knew he meant to go shooting over Mr. Braithwaite's fields that afternoon."

"Can we get any guidance from your own investigations?" asked Gill. "If we discount personal motives, the field is very wide."

"I had better explain to you, I suppose, the line I have been working on." He was fumbling in his pocket as he spoke, and produced at length an old envelope covered with pencilled scrawls, which he frowned at for a moment and then put down carefully on the desk in front of him. "I began with a somewhat arbitrary assumption: that the man I was looking for was one with an intimate knowledge of the project the Missile Division are at the moment most concerned with. We must accept, I think, that the Computer Group are in some way concerned with what has been happening.'' He disregarded the look that passed between the two policemen, and went on: ''Of the two remaining members, I must admit Naylor is the most likely as a principal in the affair. To whom we must add: Josiah Akeroyd, Basil Vlasov, John Lund, and Evan Williams. Could all those people have killed Bill Homer?''

''So far as I recollect, Mr. Akeroyd was in London. But at the time we thought the death an accident.''

''You must have made some sort of a check of cars.''

''Yes, but a general one only. We'd no evidence pointing to any particular person, you see. In any case, we found nothing.''

''I see. Then, which of those five men could have killed Weston?'' He paused, and smiled. ''Well, perhaps I'm in a better position than you are to provide an answer. Akeroyd was away for the holiday, I believe; Lund had gone to Leeds, to the pantomime; Naylor had gone to the pictures; Evan Williams, I understand, has not elaborated on his statement that he was out.''

''Most likely with Linda Carleton,'' said Gill. He coughed, and added apologetically, ''plenty of gossip around, and I expect some of it is true.''

''It is, at least, an interesting sidelight.'' He paused, as once again memory took over, producing for him a disconcertingly vivid picture. ''Basil, of course,'' he said, ''was more or less on the spot.'' He remembered, as he spoke, the mud almost ankle deep on the river path; the mist that was beginning to form down there near the water, though the town was clear. And as George slowed and said over his shoulder, ''It's just along here,'' Basil had spoken apologetically out of the darkness. ''If you're looking for Richard,'' he had said, ''I've just found him.'' The recollection had been at the forefront of his mind ever since, but it seemed to have had less effect on the two policemen, for Murray said now:

''And your friend Ramsey, for instance, when he went to look for his brother-in-law. It could have been then.''

Antony came back to the present, to the cold stuffiness of the office at the police station, to hear Gill's deep voice add with gentle persistence:

"He certainly knew where to look for him. Do you think he was really so anxious?"

Antony shook his head. His voice was carefully non-committal. "He says Ella Weston was nervous; in fairness, I should say I think it quite reasonable that he should have humoured her by going out to find her husband."

"But Ramsey is not on your short list, Mr. Maitland?"

"I suppose, in view of the way his name keeps cropping up, I should keep him in mind for my second list—possible accomplices. Apart from him, it is quite short: Dick Appleby, because he seems to spend more money than he ought to have; and Tom Burns, whose behaviour seems to suggest some knowledge he is unwilling to share. And speaking of Burns, I must admit there is an uncomfortable possibility here, which invalidates all my arguments: if *he* is the accessory, the principal is not of necessity a man with the special knowledge I have assumed."

There was a pause, while the two policemen apparently digested this information. Murray said at last: "As we seem to have got back to the Computer Group, where do you think Bill Homer came into the picture?"

"I can see three possible explanations of his death——" Antony began.

"Three?" said Murray; and his tone was sceptical.

"Certainly." He spoke firmly, but then he smiled. "Bear with me, Sergeant. Naylor's guilt is one explanation, I admit—the one you favour, isn't it?—but only one of the possibilities."

"And the other two——?"

"That Homer himself was guilty of espionage, and was killed by an associate or (less likely perhaps) by someone who discovered his treachery and killed him in an access of moral indignation. Or that he communicated some details of his work to another person, in all innocence; and later, when the information was found to have gone beyond the Missile Division, even out of the country, he realised who must have been responsible; if that happened, it was quite an adequate motive for the person concerned to dispose of him. On the other hand, if one of his colleagues— Naylor or Burns—was responsible for the leakage of information and Homer caught him out . . . well, there's your motive ready made!''

''Precisely!'' said Murray; and glanced again at Constable Gill. But Gill was watching Maitland intently, and said only:

''What else is on your mind, sir?''

''I'm guessing here . . . but it just doesn't fit. Your suspicions of Stephen Naylor are based mainly on the fact that he is the last person known to have seen Carleton the night he disappeared. But I don't believe the same person killed Carleton as killed the other two.''

''We've three different ways of killing,'' Murray pointed out. ''If that's what is bothering you.''

''Yes, well . . . leave it for now. There is one further point I should like to make: that Carleton was at the works on the night Bill Homer died——''

''I didn't know that.'' Murray spoke hurriedly, and frowned as he spoke.

''You made your inquiries at the gate-house, I expect. He wasn't in the lab, but over in the old house, talking to Sir Thomas.''

''I don't quite see——''

''No, of course, that's only half of it. When Carleton in his turn was killed (or, to be accurate, I should say the night he disappeared), Weston was also working late. And that adds up to a situation that I don't like at all.''

Murray said slowly: ''If they were killed because they knew too much . . . if one death led to another——'' He looked at Gill, who said with a grin, and a sudden lapse from his normal solemnity:

''There were a great many people in Mardingley when Weston died.''

''Yes, well.'' Antony got up. ''That seems to be about all for the moment, don't you think?''

''I suppose so.'' Murray sounded worried. ''Are you expecting——?''

"Action," said Antony. "And another death, unless I miss my guess."

"Can you do anything?"

"Not unless you're ready to charge Stephen Naylor. That might delay matters, but I doubt at this stage if you could make it stick."

"We can watch him pretty close, if that's the way it is."

"Unobtrusively," warned Antony; and looked a little doubtfully at Gill. "I don't really want to delay matters, you know. But it would be nice if we could get away without another murder."

CHAPTER TEN

BACK AT THE works, he found William Knowles stuffing papers into his brief-case. "Orders to call an emergency Board Meeting in London for to-morrow," he said, riffling the pages of a file in a distracted way, and then discarding it as irrelevant. "Trouble, dear boy . . . capital T. First rule in the book, keep the Board happy; now the Directors have got worried, the Ministry have been at them, I should say——" He broke off, and eyed his companion a trifle wistfully. "I suppose there's nothing to report," he hazarded.

Antony seated himself on the corner of the desk, and smiled at him. He had grown to like and respect Knowles during the brief period of their acquaintance, and would have been glad to speak reassuringly. "I've been talking to the police," he said. "I had to be franker with them than I like, but at least they'll do nothing to embarrass the company: not while the case remains at local level, anyway. The inference is, they'll not ask help from Central so long as I co-operate; but that won't last, of course, unless I can help them effectively."

Knowles snapped the lock of his brief-case, and sat down; he moved heavily, without his normal resilience. "*Do* you know anything?" he asked despondently, and Antony smiled again.

"Oddments," he said. "Nothing, I'm afraid, that would comfort your directors." He paused, and there was no amusement in his tone as he went on. "I'm going to ask Jenny to go back to town."

"My dear fellow!" As a comment it might seem inadequate, but Knowles's tone was full of concern. Antony got

up with an abrupt movement, and walked to the window
and stood looking out.

"I should never have let her come," he said. "I don't
think I realised——"

"That means," said Knowles shrewdly, "you think
things are going to move. Not but what you'd say three
deaths was movement enough for anybody," he added
reflectively. "But still——"

"I think," said Antony, "that George gave the game
away very effectively when he came straight to me after
finding Weston's body; the logical person would have
been one of his senior colleagues, not the stranger within
the gates."

"A small point, I should have thought."

"Not to a man already on his guard. It isn't altogether a
bad thing; it means that when I take a hand in the game I
can do so without giving away any sort of advantage." He
turned from the window, and met Knowles's worried look,
and laughed softly. "Don't tell me its dangerous. You
knew that—didn't you?—before ever you asked my help."

"I knew," said the other. "Like you . . . I didn't
realise."

"Well, don't worry about that. This 'Full Moon' project
of yours——" He stopped, because he was thinking: a
thing like that might very well be worth a man's life. He
said aloud, after a moment: "Tell the Board you'll have
the thing wrapped up within the week," and turned again
to the window. To the right was the bulk of the Technical
Block, to the left the sweep of the moor; and not for the
first time, he found comfort in its quietness.

Susie Jenner looked up from her typewriter as he went
through into her office, and smiled at him with her accustomed serenity. Antony stood near her desk, and picked up
a paper-knife to occupy his hands. "I expect this sudden
decision about the Board Meeting has made you pretty
busy," he said.

"Not too bad. The official notices went out for a date
before Christmas, you know. And Sales Department takes

care of the reservations; that's where Mickey is now—
making sure they don't get side-tracked.''

"I hope she's feeling better." He ignored Susie's startled look of inquiry and went on vaguely: "I thought she
was looking tired before the holiday."

"I believe you know very well what was the matter."
Her voice was suddenly tart, and she went on without
waiting for his protest. "Basil told me——"

"Yes?" prompted Antony gently; but his look was suddenly intent.

"He told me—it wasn't just gossip, really it wasn't!"
She flushed as she spoke, but went on with a kind of
desperation: "It was because . . . because he saw I was
worried about Stephen, and so he said I should trust you to
put things right, he thought that's why you were here."

"It seems a very odd statement." He put the paper-
knife down carefully and retreated a pace or two from the
desk so that he stood looking down at her with his back to
the light. Susie swivelled her chair so that she still faced
him, and answered firmly enough.

"No, because he says George must know about it, and
that's why he came to you when Mr. Weston was dead."

"I've known George a long time," said Antony, non-
committally. "I wonder why you should be so worried
about Stephen?" he added.

Susie's hands were clenched on the desk in front of her.
She was silent for so long that he thought she was going to
ignore the query, but then she seemed to reach a decision.
"I've no right to worry, I know; except that I used to think
that perhaps he'd some day ask me to marry him. But
there's been so much talk here; and I could tell he didn't
like the police questioning. And then, you see, there's how
Sir Thomas feels."

Antony did not pause to wonder what had induced this
sudden rush of confidences from a girl who was normally
as self-contained as Susie Jenner. It was a question he
might often have asked himself, but being as little given to
introspection as the next man he had never paused to
consider what quality he possessed that encouraged others
to talk to him. "How does Sir Thomas feel?" he asked.

Susie shook her head. "He wanted to fire Stephen," she said, as though the idea were incomprehensible to her. "I suppose he really thinks Stephen's mixed up in all this," she added, with the air of one trying desperately to be fair.

"I wonder," said Antony, "whether he has any reason——"

"He couldn't have," she interrupted, and eyed him with sudden hostility. "But it's enough to make anyone worried, even so."

"Quite enough," said Antony; and allowed, for a moment, his sympathy to be apparent in his tone. She smiled at him uncertainly, and went on, with a fair assumption of her normal manner:

"You haven't told me—and I promise I wouldn't tell anyone—you haven't said if you can help Stephen."

Antony turned his head and listened, but the footsteps he had heard went on past the office door. "I think," he said, "that Sir Thomas's attitude isn't altogether incomprehensible. Your Stephen isn't an easy man to know."

"He isn't 'my' Stephen." Susie spoke with uncharacteristic petulance. "And I don't know what you mean."

"Tell me about Mickey, then. What upset her?"

"She was in love . . . well, half in love, anyway . . . with Harry Carleton. So now she feels guilty." Her tone was that of one who states an incontrovertible fact, but her glance at him was sidelong, uneasy.

"And with a woman's genius for turning every issue into a personal one she thinks, I suppose, that Tom Burns killed Carleton for the sake of her bright eyes," said Antony roughly. "Haven't you a particle of sense between you?" He met her startled look with an angry one, but went on more gently: "This is no time for discretion, Susie Jenner. If you know anything——"

"I don't seem to have been very discreet so far," said Susie ruefully. "And you never told me if Basil was right. But I think I'd better trust you." She paused, and produced an unfemininely large white handkerchief, and blew her nose in a business-like way that her companion found both absurd and touching. "I think Mickey thought—what you said—or something like it. And I did wonder about

Tom: whether perhaps he might have found out something about Bill and Harry, and the way he felt about Mickey made it seem worse. I mean, Harry *was* a cad, you can't get away from that. He only took Mickey out two or three times, and she shouldn't have gone with him, of course; and I don't suppose he knew, or cared, the effect it had on her. But none of that explains about Mr. Weston."

"You said," Antony remarked, "that you were going to trust me." He saw her flush, and turned his head, and did not look at her as she went on.

"About Stephen." Her voice was strained, and she stopped to clear her throat, but then went on more resolutely. "When Sir Thomas and Mr. Akeroyd were arguing about him, Sir Thomas said he suspected Stephen because of something Harry had told him . . . something that happened the night Bill died. I know that's true, because Miss Macaulay heard some of what they said—they were shouting, you know; but I don't know any more. I didn't want to tell you, because it sounds as if I thought Stephen might have done something wrong; but I do see that if you knew all that Harry said it might help you." (Antony spared a moment's rueful thought for the fact that his evasions seemed to have had no effect whatever on the idea that Basil had planted in her head.) "And though I think Stephen . . . well, I suppose he *might* kill somebody in anger; but not like Bill was killed, or Mr. Weston . . . not thinking it out, you know. And as for believing he's a spy——!" She had talked herself into a sort of calmness, and her scornful tone underlined the absurdity of the idea. "I only hope," she added, uneasily, "that I've done right to tell you."

Antony hoped so too; he had done his best to give his mind to what she told him, but felt in no case to judge its importance. He left her presently, and went across the landing to Miss Macaulay's office in a disturbed and anxious frame of mind.

Miss Macaulay was helpful, and Sir Thomas (surprisingly) free. He looked up and scowled as Antony went into his room, and remarked belligerently: "I expected your report as soon as you left the police. But Ambler tells me you've been in since about ten-thirty.''

"About that," Antony agreed.

"Well, now that you are here, what had they to say? Are they ready to make an arrest?" His tone was hectoring, but it seemed likely that this attitude covered a good deal of uneasiness.

"Not just yet, I think."

"The more fools they! And why not, I should like to know?"

"Lack of evidence," said Antony, who knew perfectly well that the question was rhetorical; and added, still with intent to annoy: "But I came to ask for information, not to give it."

"Ha?" said Sir Thomas, angrily. "I seem to remember telling you——"

"In case you've forgotten, sir, you're not in a position to 'tell' me anything. You can throw me out of the firm," he conceded, as the other man's look became positively ferocious, "but you'll have trouble with the police if you do, I'll tell you that much. And I don't imagine your Board will be over-pleased."

"Are you threatening me, young man?" Antony's gesture disclaimed to some degree this intention, and Sir Thomas added, in an over-wrought way: "All right, all right, what do you want to know?"

"First, what have you got against Stephen Naylor?"

"Well, good lord, if that isn't obvious! It was his section, wasn't it, where all the trouble started? And Carleton told me himself somebody was waiting for Bill Homer; that was not long after Stephen left the laboratory, let me remind you. And if anybody had an opportunity for making away with Harry Carleton——"

"Akeroyd doesn't agree with you," Antony pointed out. Sir Thomas snorted.

"Sentimental old fool!" he said; and Antony found himself lingering momentarily on the reflection of how surprised and indignant Josiah would have been on hearing this description. "If a man has technical ability, that's all that counts with him," Sir Thomas went on. "Important, of course," he admitted. "But so far as liking is concerned . . . I find him unbearably surly. Of course, Josiah knew his parents."

"Did he, indeed?" Antony found this of interest, but did not linger over the information. "There was another appointment you disagreed over," he said. "Richard Weston."

Sir Thomas stared at him. "Well, if that don't beat cock fighting!" he said at length. "Akeroyd couldn't stand him, said he didn't know the job. Couldn't be true, you know, the Research Department has been notably successful on this project."

"I was told——"

"Yes, of course. But several people thought *they* should have been promoted; one of the reasons I brought Weston in, actually, two people with equal claims. So it's no wonder there was talk." He seemed to be talking himself into a better temper, but the look he directed at his companion was one of calculation, as though he were wondering just how specious his explanations really sounded. Antony ignored the look, and reverted without warning to his original theme.

"What, exactly, did Harry Carleton tell you about the night Homer died?"

The question seemed to be a disconcerting one. "Why . . . nothing but what I told you."

"You said 'somebody was waiting for Bill Homer.' Well, how did Carleton know that? What did he hear . . . or see?"

Sir Thomas reflected. "As to seeing . . . nothing. You couldn't, that night. He said he strolled away from the main door, where he was waiting for me, and encountered one of his colleagues—almost bumped into him, in fact. He said that, later, this man had not mentioned his presence to anyone else, but had given him a good reason for not wanting it to be known. He said, now he was wondering should he have agreed to keep silence? Harry was like that, you know . . . loved to stir up trouble."

"Did he say it was Stephen he saw?"

"I asked him that, naturally. He neither confirmed nor

denied it, but I was certainly left with the impression——"
(An odd man, Antony thought; honest enough to recount
what he had been told without embellishment, not quite
honest enough to realise the presence in himself of preju-
dices which should be discounted.) "And who more likely?"
said Sir Thomas, more belligerently. "After all——" (After all, the evidence could be dangerous to Stephen; it
didn't need to be conclusive, just another indication——)

Jenny listened gravely to what he had to say, but shook
her head when Antony finished speaking. "I don't think
you're being very sensible, darling. What do you think
may happen?"

"I should have thought that was obvious. Oh, well, I
don't know, I suppose. If I did, I wouldn't be so anxious." He had been prowling up and down the room as he
spoke, but now he stopped and stood looking down at her,
trying—and not now very hopefully—to convince her of
the rightness of what he was saying. "I think we must take
it, at least," he added, "that my present employment is no
longer of any use as camouflage."

"I expect you're right about that," said Jenny. She was
darning, and paused to re-thread her needle; as though, her
husband thought a trifle resentfully, her calmness needed
any demonstration. "But if what you've told me about the
person you want is also correct——"

"Dammit, Jenny, I don't know——" he protested.

"Well, of course not. But you've told me a lot about
him, and you must admit he always seems to have a
motive for what he does."

"What is a motive to A, is stark lunacy to B. *That's* no
argument." Antony sat down on the edge of the bed, and
pushed his fingers through his hair. "In words of one
syllable, my love, I'm not too worried about whoever-it-is-
at-the-factory . . . not on your account. But there's an
organisation behind him, and that does frighten me."

"They're just as likely to be in London as in Yorkshire,
so what's the use of sending me home?" said Jenny,
triumphantly. "As a matter of fact, I'll be much safer
here, because Mrs. Ambler is in most of the time, and if

she goes shopping I can easily go too; but in London I might be alone all day." Antony was looking at her blankly, and she added with a little hesitation: "I'll go—of course—if my being here is going to upset you."

"I'll be worried to death either way now," he admitted. "I should never——"

"Then it's my decision, and I shall stay," said Jenny firmly. "I shan't do anything silly, you know."

"I know," said Antony. He did not sound much comforted by the assurance, and after a moment she added, quietly:

"If it were just the danger, I'd run away like anything. At least," she added, honestly, "I might. But it's the—the horridness. I didn't understand about that, and I think I ought to know——"

"All right, love, we'll see it through together." Not for the first time in his life, Antony regretted momentarily a sense of fair play that would not allow him to ask her to accept a lower standard than the one he set for himself. What she said was true enough, of course. But it neither convinced nor consoled him.

CHAPTER ELEVEN

THERE WAS AN understanding among George's circle at Carcroft that he and his wife kept open house for their friends on Thursday evenings. This week, however, it was known that Beryl would be with her sister-in-law, and the group that was assembled was, therefore, exclusively male and predominantly bachelor. Antony, leaving Jenny to spend the evening with the Amblers, found Basil shrugging into his coat in the hall of Holly Royd.

"If you're going to George's I'll walk with you," he offered. Basil favoured him with his sleepy smile.

"I was afraid you might," he said. And added, as soon as the front door was closed behind them, "You've been talking to Susie Jenner, I shouldn't wonder."

"From what she tells me, you seem to have jumped to a rather remarkable conclusion," said Antony mildly.

"I don't jump to conclusions." Basil's tone was definite. "Far too much effort involved. But in this case there was no need, I assure you . . . general talk in the lab . . . just following the herd, old boy."

"You don't, surely, believe all you hear?"

"Oh, no. But George was denying it so strenuously——"

"Damn George!" said Maitland, with feeling.

"Well, if you like. It seems a little late to think of that now, though," Basil pointed out. They walked on in silence for a while; it was cold still, but clear, and not unpleasant for walking. Basil said, at last, with an air of innocent relish; "Not my business, of course, but you *are* getting your money's worth, aren't you?"

Antony laughed reluctantly. "I suppose it's no use my denying——?"

"Not a bit. Heard it all already, from George. And I don't see that it matters, anyway."

"Don't you?" said Antony grimly. "Don't you, indeed?"

"Not really," said the other. "After all, we all know now someone's spying. Stands to reason something's being done about it."

It struck Maitland then that for the first time he was talking to someone who expressed neither surprise nor horror at what was happening. He said slowly: "Doesn't it seem odd to you that one of your colleagues——?"

"If your name were Vlasov, even though your family had been in England for sometime, you would have learned—in self defence—a good deal about the Communists. I am not so naïve as to imagine that what we are doing has escaped their attention." His tone was matter-of-fact, no bitterness, certainly no self-pity. Antony glanced at him curiously as they passed beneath a street lamp, and saw his face as calm as ever.

"They say every man has his price," he said; and made the words a question.

Basil laughed. "A half-truth," he said lightly. "At least . . . the price is not always money."

"I suppose not," said Antony discontentedly. "But I don't think that helps me."

"Well, let's see." Basil had reverted to his dreamy tone. "Sir Thomas's price would be power, I think . . . not very original, I'm sorry," he added apologetically.

"Do you know his background?" the other asked with interest.

"Ah, that's rather more *recherché*. He's proud of being a self-made man, but you mustn't be imagining a meteoric rise from the gutter: good middle-class stock and a grammar school education . . . but nothing to lead automatically to his present job, of course. The title was tacked on at the end of the war, but he dislikes the historical associations so much I'm surprised he accepted it."

"I don't see why."

"My own view is, he can't bear to think he shares his name, even with a poor so-and-so who was murdered in the seventeenth century. However . . . Josiah now; *his* price would be complete freedom of action, no interference whatever . . . and nobody would be likely to pay him that.'' They had reached George's gate as he was speaking, and he had halted in the drive to finish his remarks. ''And my price, my dear Maitland,'' he added over his shoulder, as he went up the steps to the front door, ''my price would be something in the nature of greater mental capacity. Stephen would no doubt suggest equipping me with a large and omniscient computer . . . which reminds me! Is it *your* idea that Stephen should have a watch-dog?''

George opened the door before Antony could reply, and he didn't know whether to be glad or sorry. Basil's discourse was undeniably illuminating; and if his penetration was sometimes disconcerting, as he said himself—what did it matter?

George looked worried, a not unusual state with him these days. He greeted Basil with pleasure, Antony with a doubtful look, and led the way back to his sitting-room, a big room on the left of the hall. This also was a stone house, though less massively built than Holly Royd and furnished, of course, at a much later date. The result might be unimaginative, but was undeniably comfortable; and what, thought Antony—sinking gratefully into a vast armchair—what could be more desirable than that?

Two men had already arrived, John Lund and Dick Appleby; and John had brought with him his fifteen-year-old son, whose school holidays were not yet over. Johnny Lund was an attractive boy, as tall and good-looking as his father, but with a certain gentleness of manner which Maitland, watching him in the first moments of their acquaintance, put down as an inheritance from his mother. The boy came across to speak to him, which at first he thought a pleasant touch of deference towards the only stranger present; but after a moment he began to wonder. Certainly, Johnny was a well-mannered youngster, but his questions had a purpose: he wanted to know whatever there was to tell about the legal profession in general and the Bar in particular. Antony, torn between his outworn role of failure and his natural disinclination to abandon it, played down his answers and, looking up, found Basil eyeing him with a sardonic expression. Johnny, at his elbow, said earnestly:

"I do find it interesting, sir, hearing about something besides engineering. I mean, that's interesting too, but I want to know about . . . about everything."

"That's a tall order," said Antony, amused. "By the way, how did you enjoy the pantomime?"

"It was splendid!" There could be no doubt about his enthusiasm. "There was a man with a donkey . . . well, it wasn't really a donkey, of course, though I don't really see why you shouldn't have a real one. Mrs. Foster said——" He paused, and—as Antony put it later—grew up under his eyes. "It was all very childish, you know," he said. "But you were telling me——"

Antony returned obligingly to his legal anecdotes, as being comparatively safe ground. After a while George moved across the room to join them, and he realised that his audience was now enlarged and finished off what he was saying rather abruptly. Johnny gave him a grateful smile, in which there was also something of the conspirator, and moved across to the bookcase in the corner. Ramsey looked after him and said—speaking to Antony, but including Lund in the conversation:

"There's a lad that's going to take the shine out of our Research Department, Antony. One scholarship after another; hoping for Cambridge, aren't you, John?"

"Hoping," said Lund. "I want the best for Johnny, but he'll have to make up his mind——"

"There's plenty of time yet," said George. And Basil, who had propped himself up comfortably in the corner of the sofa, said sleepily:

"That would be John's price, Antony. Unlimited opportunity for technical progress." George seemed a little startled by this pronouncement; but Lund, more used to his colleague's vagaries, merely looked inquiringly, first at the speaker—who seemed already to be asleep again—and then at Antony, who explained briefly.

"We were discussing as we walked here the old saying, that every man has his price."

"That's an amusing thought," said Appleby. "What's yours, I wonder?"

"Peace of mind, I should think," said Antony, conscious suddenly that the room was too warm and that the situation was difficult and wearing. Basil opened both eyes, and remarked with a disconcerting effect of alertness:

"My price would be a better brain, we decided that. What about you, Dick? Wine, women and song?" Appleby grinned at him. "Well, not song, perhaps—hardly fair to the rest of us. Let's say—whatever it is takes you to Harrogate so often."

There was, for a moment, an uncomfortable stillness about the little group. Then Dick laughed, uneasily, and Basil went on in his imperturbable way: "As for George—do you know?—I think he must be the exception that proves the rule. I don't believe there's anything he wants enough to——"

"Perhaps," said George, "I've already got what I want." And again the silence had a quality of coldness. Afterwards Antony could picture the group vividly: George, stout and anxious, but with something in his expression . . . a suggestion of slyness, of self-satisfaction; Basil, somnolent again, but it wouldn't take much to rouse him if his interest were caught; Lund, a big man, almost imperturbable . . . almost, not quite; and Appleby, elaborately unconcerned, feeling for his cigarette case . . . a stolid young man who seemed inexplicably to have been shaken by a casual remark. But, reviewing this comprehensive picture later and at leisure, Maitland doubted very much whether any of Basil Vlasov's remarks that evening had been other than deliberate.

That, however, was later. Just then there was the little group of men, awkwardly self-conscious; and Lund's voice cutting calmly through the silence. "How is Ella, George?"

"Not too good." Ramsey's shake of the head and lugubrious tone were completely natural; the moment of strain passed, here was only a normal gathering of familiar friends. A sad occasion, certainly; George enlarged on that for a while, as might have been expected. He was interrupted by the front-door bell, and left with a muttered apology, to return a moment later ushering Stephen Naylor in front of him. There was a chorus of greeting, and then somebody asked:

"Where's Evan, I thought he was coming?"

Appleby had evidently heard the same rumours as had Constable Gill, for he said with a grin: "Courting, I shouldn't wonder."

"More likely to be outside somewhere, shadowing me," Basil remarked. And Lund laughed, though not as though the subject amused him.

"Don't tell me that bee's still buzzing. Surely you could do something about it, Basil."

"Who me?" said Basil, injured. "Well, what?" he demanded.

"You might, for instance," Antony suggested, "have told him what you'd like to achieve with that 'better brain' we were talking about."

"Meaning . . . you'd like to know?" asked Dick Appleby.

"I should, very much," said Antony. Stephen had crossed the room to where Johnny Lund was still browsing in the 1914 *Punch*, but he said now over his shoulder:

"Knowledge for knowledge's sake."

"But I'd hate to disillusion Evan," said Basil, nodding in apparent agreement. "It does him good to have an interest."

Dick had been over to the side table to refill his glass of beer, and now came to stand behind Antony's chair; he said, with something like a sneer: "So you can stop worrying about that, can't you?"

Antony turned a little to look up at him. "I wasn't, particularly," he said mildly. "But, talking about worrying, it might be healthy for you to indulge the emotion a little. To the extent, at least, of taking care—" Dick stared at him blankly, and then laughed.

"The gypsy's warning," he said. "So the chaps were right who said you were the management's tame sleuth!"

Maitland did not attempt to deny it. He said, seriously: "This isn't a parlour game, Appleby. Three men have died——"

"And I'm to be the fourth?"

"That isn't what I said," Antony objected. Dick drained his glass and placed it on the table behind him. When he turned to look down at the other man again his expression was hard to read, and he said almost pettishly:

"I can't see why you should take it so seriously. What is there to be worried about? They know it all, anyway, don't they?"

"Perhaps not quite all." Antony seemed to be giving the question careful consideration, then he looked up again at the other man and smiled. "But even granting your premise there remains—doesn't there?—the little matter of where your loyalties lie."

"You make me sick!" said Appleby. He seemed to become aware suddenly that they were not alone, and turned on his heel and went quickly out of the room. A moment later they heard the front door slam. Basil gave a faint moan, as though in protest at this display of energy.

"What on earth was all that?" he murmured.

"Never mind Dick." Lund brushed the episode aside, and as usual seemed concerned with restoring a semblance, at least, of normality. "I've been meaning to ask you, Antony, about this Board Meeting——"

"There seems to be some concern," said Maitland, at his driest, "about the events at Carcroft. The Board don't like it, naturally; and, what's more to the point, the Ministry have got the wind up."

"I suppose that was inevitable," said Lund, reflectively. "But it could be damned awkward, just now."

Antony glanced across at Stephen, who had been taking no part in the conversation, and wondered—not for the first time since the younger man arrived—what had happened to upset him still further. Just for a moment, however, his anxieties seemed to be forgotten. He looked to be in a blaze of excitement. "It doesn't——" he said; and then, changing his mind: "Oh, well, forget it!"

John Lund's look was a nice blend of amusement and exasperation. "What's biting you, Stephen?" he demanded.

"Nothing . . . really! I'll tell you one thing, though: the

police have turned up a witness who saw Harry's car, the night he disappeared——''

"Where was that?" asked Maitland sharply.

"At Dangerous Corner—do you know it?—going towards Harrogate."

"Well, that makes sense, anyway," said Antony, with an air of relief. "Are they sure——?"

"Oh, yes. Harry drove a Morris, but it had some rather—er—singular defects," Stephen explained. "Hadn't it?" he appealed to the others. But only George murmured a polite response. The attention of the others had been fixed by Maitland's remark.

"What makes sense?" asked Lund quietly; and:

"Where do you suppose he was going?" Basil inquired.

"Taking the quickest route to the North Yorkshire moors, I'd say. And I don't suppose Carleton was driving." As he spoke, he became aware that Johnny had put down his book and come back to join the group. The boy had an anxious look, and Antony continued less directly. "They're big, you know, none of your fiddling little moors. And I know a farm where they have a genuine bog, just outside the yard gate. They lost a tractor in it once; that made them think."

"I should think it might," said George.

"Yes, but it had its uses, too. It saved them the expense of keeping a pack of dogs——" He was watching Johnny's face as he spoke, had seen anxiety change to plain bewilderment, and now the boy laughed aloud.

"I've read books like that," he said. "Any stranger goes near—grr—they set the dogs on him!"

"Was that what your friends did?" inquired Basil, faintly.

"No, I told you, they sent them to join the tractor. The trouble was, though, whenever there was a fog one of the family always fell into the bog too, and was never seen again. And at last there was only one of them left."

"What happened to him?" asked Johnny.

"No one thought he'd mind. He was one of those strong, silent men, and never did anything but grunt, anyway. But the lack of someone to be silent at seemed to prey on his mind. *He* hanged himself in the barn."

The story was well received, the hint was taken, and the problems of General Aircraft were not returned to until after the Lunds had left. Basil had gone some minutes before, and when Ramsey came back into the sitting-room he found his two remaining guests already deep in conversation.

Stephen had come to the point without any preamble at all. "I've been talking to Tom Burns," he said.

Antony looked inquiring. "And you didn't like what he had to say?" he hazarded.

"I did not!" Stephen pondered a moment, and his face was flushed as he went on. "I know there's been talk in the lab, but people will, you know. It doesn't mean much, you can forget it. And I'm pretty sure what the police think, of course. But I know Tom rather well, you see."

"You're trying to tell me that Burns has accused you——?"

"Well, not exactly. We were working late, but I stayed behind; I wanted to do some final runs, you know, without anyone knowing the results."

"That seems reasonable."

"I think so. But Tom didn't like it. He gave me a queerish look, so I asked him——" He broke off, as George came into the room again, but went on in a moment without prompting. "He was with Miss Macaulay when Josiah and the M.D. were having that row. Well, I knew Sir Thomas had it in for me . . . but, Tom!"

"From what I know of that conversation," said Antony, "I shouldn't blame him too much for getting a wrong impression. Sir Thomas construed something Harry Carleton told him as meaning that he had spoken to you here, the night Homer was killed, and some time after you were supposed to have gone home."

"That just isn't true!"

"Probably not. I think that perhaps Carleton deliberately tried to foster that impression, doubtless for his own ends."

"He was a born mischief-maker," George put in. Stephen looked at him gratefully.

"Then you don't think——"

"I've a weakness for proof," said Antony.

Stephen said angrily: "I don't just want the benefit of the doubt." Maitland looked at him without speaking. "I want . . . oh, lord, I wish the whole blasted business was over!"

"You can say that again," said George, with feeling. "Did you talk to Tom?"

"I did." A note of satisfaction sounded in his voice. "I told him just what I thought of him, so I think he realised——"

"After all," Antony put in, apologetically, "he might just as well have taken umbrage when you wanted to do your runs on the computer without him there." Stephen gave him a helpless look, and then grinned with genuine amusement. "Yes, I thought that hadn't occurred to you," he added.

They went into the kitchen after that, and washed the glasses that had been used, and made a companionable pot of tea. George had reverted to the question Lund had raised about the Board Meeting, and was worrying away at the subject like a dog with a bone he does not relish, but can't bear to be parted from. Stephen seemed to have recovered his spirits, and was humming to himself as he found a tea-towel and rubbed the glasses until he was satisfied with the resultant shine. After a while, finding Maitland's eyes fixed on him reflectively, the tune died away and he asked:

"How long do you think I've got?" And when Antony opened his mouth to reply with a question, added impatiently: "Before the police . . . do anything drastic, I mean."

"At a guess, I should say we both have about four days . . . if we live that long, of course." George gave a shocked exclamation; Stephen was eyeing him frowningly. "I told Knowles a week, the Ministry won't wait that long, of course. And when they start pressing, the police won't wait any longer for action from me."

"And 'Full Moon' will go on the scrap heap," said George. "Lord knows what John Lund will make of that."

"Is he specially concerned?"

"Not really, but he was on that 'Grass Snake' thing that

was cancelled three years back . . . nobody likes to be on a project that folds up, you know." He spoke lugubriously, but Stephen wasn't listening.

"Four days," he was saying; and it occurred to Antony that the words sounded almost like a prayer. "Four days should do it." He looked up, and the gleam of excitement was back in his eye. "They wouldn't cancel the project if we could prove it was successful," he said.

Antony put down his cup with a clatter on the kitchen table. "Those runs you were doing?" he said. "For heaven's sake, Stephen——"

"Don't worry, I had the recordings burned. I need a few more days; the only thing is, the police are following me, I was afraid that meant——"

"Well, you see," said Antony, "I asked them to."

Naylor did not reply for a moment. He hung the tea-towel on its appointed rail, straightening it carefully, and then came to the table and poured himself a second cup of tea. At last he said: "Does that mean you think I'm guilty?" And though he spoke as though he were choosing his words, he did not sound resentful.

"It means, I think these events would stop—if only for a time—if you were under arrest," said Antony. "That could be because you are directly responsible for what has happened; or it could be that you've been elected scape-goat."

George gave again his inarticulate moan of protest, and then added more coherently: "You mean, right from the beginning . . . when Stephen's letter was taken, that was a—a frame-up?"

"Oh, no, somebody wanted to read it, all right. It was too easy, to hide it for the time; and then photograph it, I suppose, and replace it at leisure. You all work pretty odd hours, there's nothing in somebody being alone in the lab."

"Easy?" said Stephen, pensively. "I don't see——"

"Well, I don't know, of course; but if I'd been hiding it . . . I think if you look you'll find traces of Scotch tape on the underside of one of the desks. You'd look under them when you were searching, and move them away from the wall, and so on; but I bet nobody thought of lying flat on the floor and looking up.''

"No, as a matter of fact——''

"Nobody thought of that," said Stephen. He seemed to be going back over the conversation. "And talking of thinking of things . . . I suppose you checked with the gate house to see who was last in the lab that night?''

"Evan Williams," said Antony promptly. "He stayed about half an hour longer than the rest of you. But both Dick and Basil came back during the evening, and were alone in the lab for twenty and thirty-five minutes respectively." He looked from one to other of his companions: Stephen's expression was stony, but George looked thoroughly shocked, and just for the moment Antony allowed himself to realise, and sympathise with, their feelings. "It isn't conclusive," he pointed out gently. "But once the report got into the system, as it were, there'd never be so good a chance again . . . even for you, Stephen.''

"No, I see that," said Stephen slowly. "If the various things have been recorded on microfilm, they'd be easy enough to get away with.''

"But, for some reason, you don't believe it was Stephen," said George. "Do you?" he challenged. Maitland drained his cup and got to his feet.

"I don't *think* so," he admitted. "But I can't afford to play my hunches, you must see that.''

Jenny was sitting up in bed, reading, when he got back to Holly Royd. Antony kicked the fire into a blaze, and went to sit on the edge of the bed. His wife moved her feet obligingly, and put down her book. "Did you tell me once that Mardingley does its week-end shopping on Friday morning?" he asked unexpectedly.

"Oh, yes, if I go with Mrs. Ambler we meet *everybody* on Friday," Jenny agreed. She showed no surprise at the question; and though her tone was encouraging, it hid her curiosity well enough.

"Then, do you think you could persuade her to do a job for me? I expect she even knows which shops people use, and where to find people.''

"What's the trouble, darling?"

"Alibis," said Antony. "For Boxing Day. That'd be the hotel people for Josiah . . . was he really away from Mardingley? Evan Williams says he was out, so I expect Linda Carleton would be the best bet . . . a bit tricky, that. John Lund's housekeeper, Mrs. Foster . . . did he really go to Leeds? Something Johnny said made me wonder. There's nothing much we can do about Stephen, and George and Basil were on the spot anyway. But I'd like to be sure about the others."

"Yes, I see. It might take longer than just one morning, you know."

"I suppose it might. Can you persuade Mrs. Ambler——?"

"That part's all right, I think. Between us——"

"Yes," said Antony, "that's what I was afraid of. Don't do anything silly, love."

"Of course not," said Jenny. "No one," she added, firmly, "could possibly suspect Mrs. Ambler of any . . . any funny business." On reflection, her husband was inclined to agree with her.

CHAPTER TWELVE

THE NEXT DAY was Friday, and the Managing Director and Company Secretary had already got back from London. Knowles greeted Antony with a troubled look. "Had the devil's own job with the Ministry, dear boy," he informed him. "Gave 'em my assurance none of the information had been collated . . . nothing concrete for anyone to get their hands on. Even so . . . five days was the best I could do, and they weren't really happy about that."

Antony, thinking of Stephen's radiant look of the evening before, was looking rather grim as he made his way across to the Missile Division a few moments later. He ran Naylor to earth eventually in Basil's office, waving a slide-rule in what might easily have been construed as a threatening way, and demanding the results of some calculations which—he said—should have been available days since. Basil smiled at him sadly, but refused to be drawn into argument. Altogether, Maitland's coming seemed to have resolved a deadlock; Stephen went with him willingly enough.

Tom Burns was in the computer room as they passed through, attending with his customary loving care to GADA's needs. He did not look up as they passed, though he muttered a greeting; but Antony had an impression that he was more at peace with the world this morning, and did not change his mind even when, looking back from the doorway of Stephen's cubby-hole, he observed that Tom had a bruised cheek-bone and a fine black eye. He was grinning as he went into the little room and shut the door firmly behind him. Stephen, who still seemed ruffled from his talk with Basil, eyed him sourly.

"Coming in here looking like a blasted Cheshire cat," he grumbled. And then, reverting to his grievance: "Passive non-co-operation," he said, and seemed a little cheered by the phrase. "Basil, of all people."

"I should say it's inevitable," said Antony. "But I shouldn't take it personally, if I were you." Stephen took his time to consider this remark, and grimaced as the implications struck him.

"Oh, well!" he said. And shrugged.

"I came," said Maitland, changing the subject firmly, "to talk to you about these test runs of yours. You're sure of your facts?"

"It'll work," said Stephen positively, "when they come to try it out."

"And who knows that . . . besides yourself?"

"Josiah would, normally. And John, as Chief Development Engineer; and the Chief Research Engineer, of course. Probably Willie and the M.D. as well. But—you see how it is: we had some 'bugs' to get out of the design. The work has been done, but only the computer runs so far show it has been done successfully. *I* haven't told anyone. Though I wouldn't mind betting Basil has a very good idea how things stand. He's nobody's fool, you know."

Antony took three steps to the window, three steps back, which was the maximum movement the little room allowed. "I hope you've enough sense," he said, "to go on keeping it under your hat. Unless you'd care to have a one-way ticket to Moscow purchased on your behalf." Naylor looked startled, and he added irritably, "I've been put to quite enough trouble over this business already. And I've no desire at all to have to involve myself in a trip to Russia; for one thing, I don't know the language."

Stephen laughed suddenly. "I believe you'd take it on, at that," he remarked. "But I shouldn't like Jenny to be worried, as she would be if you took off for the ends of the earth, so I can see I'd better take care."

"Thank you," said Antony; he did not sound grateful, and removed himself without further ado.

Upstairs, he found Josiah and Sir Thomas together in the latter's office. Akeroyd was sitting at the long table they used for meetings, his head in his hands, a picture of dejection. The Managing Director appeared to be delivering himself of a harangue. Maitland heard his own name as he pushed open the door from the landing (only Chief Executives used it as a rule, but he was in no mood this morning to trouble himself with the niceties of industrial etiquette); so he wasn't surprised when the older man turned on him immediately with bitter words. Josiah raised his head, and said in the accents he only assumed when he was deeply moved (or, occasionally, for his own amusement):

"Nay, let the lad be. He's done thee no harm."

"And no good either," said Sir Thomas, spitefully. "I've had to sit there and listen to Knight and the others prosing on; while our so-called 'expert' won't even deign to report."

Antony had crossed the room now. He stood with his hands resting lightly on the top bar of one of the ladder-backed chairs which surrounded the table. He said: "It's not so easy as that, sir, knowing who I should report to . . . knowing who I can trust." He might have said—and given less provocation—that, though he was there by courtesy of the management, his responsibility was to the Ministry of Supply; but somehow, whenever he encountered Sir Thomas, his last concern was to be in any way conciliatory.

Josiah looked up, and there was amusement in his eyes as he turned towards his colleague. Sir Thomas was staring. He said, slowly: "You dare say that . . . to my face?" And then, with more energy: "Get out!"

"It's too late for that," said Antony. "This business has got to be cleared up before . . . Tuesday is the deadline, isn't it?"

"That's it," rumbled Akeroyd. He sounded both enthusiastic and appreciative. "Knowles said *he* asked for a week," he added to Sir Thomas, who nodded without taking his eyes off Maitland's face.

"Well. Can you do it?" he asked.

"I don't know. That's not a question one can ever answer. But if I can't, you'll be out of business."

"And they'll have stopped development of one of the best ideas——" said Akeroyd. He broke off as Antony shook his head. But Sir Thomas interrupted before anything more could be said.

"At least you must admit it's too dangerous now to keep Naylor in the lab any longer," he maintained.

"I don't see that," said Josiah. "I don't see it at all." He spoke with an effect of stubbornness, but as though he had very little hope of being heeded. Antony looked slowly from one to other of the older men.

"I can give you no opinion as to his guilt or innocence," he informed them. "But the last thing you should do is sack him now."

"Why not?" Sir Thomas demanded, belligerently.

"Because I prefer to keep him under my eye. Because I think (though I may be wrong about this) that the decision would be an unjust one." He was watching the other man closely as he spoke, but seeing no change of expression added casually: "If neither of those points weighs with you, because at the moment he knows more about the action of 'Full Moon' than anybody else; it's all in his head, you may as well let him stay."

Josiah banged his fist on the table. "That last lot of tests!" he exclaimed. "He told me the results were negative, but I might have guessed——" He looked at Antony inquiringly. "The young devil; do you suppose he suspects *me*?" he asked. His tone was rather pleased than otherwise, and Maitland did not trouble to voice a disclaimer. Instead, he turned to the Managing Director.

"What do you say, sir?" he asked.

Sir Thomas shrugged his shoulders, and said a trifle fretfully: "Oh, very well!" He looked at his colleague and added in a sour tone: "I can't see what you've got to look so pleased about."

"Full Moon," said Akeroyd. He spoke raptly, and without any hesitation at all, but rather as if he were talking to himself. "That's team work for you," he added. "They're good lads, the lot of 'em."

"All but one," said Sir Thomas; and seemed visibly cheered to be introducing a discordant note into the conversation. "Don't you agree?" he added, turning suddenly to Maitland . . . demanding his co-operation calmly, for all the world as though here was an opinion he valued.

"I'm afraid I think you're underestimating." If an element of unease were to be introduced, perhaps he could do something in that line himself. "And talking of my report," he went on without awaiting comment, "do you wish me to confine myself to the question of espionage, or shall I cover the other irregularities?"

Sir Thomas scowled at him. "Irregularities?" he repeated harshly. "What the hell do you mean?" Antony grinned at him, but managed to infuse a note of apology into his reply.

"It's so difficult to draw the line——"

"Say what you mean, young man, and don't palter," Josiah commanded.

"Well then . . . blackmail," said Antony. "It's hard to see how a thing like that can be ignored in a place as vitally concerned with security as this is."

If he was looking for a reaction, Josiah's was all that could have been desired or expected. He got to his feet slowly, and leaned across the table with both fists resting on the polished surface; and for the first time since he had known him, Maitland acquitted him of any trace of intention as his accent broadened. "That sounds a moocky business," he said, "but it's nobbut a word, when all's said. What doost mean, lad?"

"I mean, I think that both Carleton and Weston were killed because of something they knew. Carleton, I've been told, was a mischief-maker; but Richard Weston, I believe, had a deeper purpose in disclosing—to one person only—what he knew."

"I don't see," said Sir Thomas flatly, "how you make that out."

"It seems to follow," said Antony, "from the fact that he was already blackmailing two—and probably three—members of the firm." He did not attempt to elaborate the statement, but Akeroyd sat down again, heavily, as though he were tired.

"George hated his guts," he said.

"So he did," agreed Sir Thomas. His eyes were fixed on Maitland's face with a fierce air of concentration. "And the other men?" he demanded. "Are they in the lab?"

"One perhaps. As for the other, I was wondering," said Antony, meeting his look, "why you chose Weston for that particular job, sir."

There was a moment of almost complete silence; so that Miss Macaulay's typewriter could be heard, clicking busily in the next room, and Antony became conscious, for the first time, of a slight humming from the electric clock. Then Josiah Akeroyd twisted in his chair to look up at his colleague; an almost comical look of inquiry. Sir Thomas ignored him, and said quietly:

"That was acute of you. How did you guess?"

"Rather belatedly, I'm afraid. Until he was killed, I'd have bet fairly heavily on Weston's being guilty of a much more serious crime. Afterwards . . . well, he still might have been involved, but I began thinking of the other queer things about him . . . looking for a motive, you know. His relationship with Ramsey was not normal, even allowing for a certain amount of mutual dislike. And when I considered his position in the firm——"

"I was not," said Sir Thomas—throwing in the remark with a deliberately casual air, "I was not in Mardingley during the Christmas holiday."

"No, sir." He hid his amusement at what might well have been regarded as an admission of weakness, and went on seriously enough. "To go back to what I was saying, I saw the list of Christmas bonuses. Lund was down for the same amount as Weston, which was reasonable; but the sums involved were disproportionate, and as Knowles disclaimed responsibility it seemed it must be your doing. For another thing—you're not a fool, sir. Yet you had the best advice at your disposal . . . and ignored it."

Sir Thomas said, unsmiling: "Take a bow, Josiah. And if I admit your allegation—which still seems to me to be made on rather flimsy grounds—if I admit it, what then?"

"I should need to be assured that there was no connection——"

"There wasn't, of course. There couldn't have been."
He spoke quietly, but stopped as Antony shook his head.
"My word, I suppose, is worth nothing. I don't see how I
can prove what I say."

Akeroyd got up again. He moved clumsily, and did not
look at his colleague. "I'll go," he muttered; and began to
move towards the door. Sir Thomas's voice stopped him in
his tracks, the words icily formal.

"Do not disturb yourself on my account; though no
doubt—like myself—you have work to do. As for this
suggestion of yours, Maitland: you may do as you please,
I have nothing to add."

"Very well, sir." Antony saw no profit, at this stage, in
starting a wrangle. "May I take it you have reconsidered
your decision with regard to Stephen Naylor?"

"Take what you like, and go to hell!" invited Sir
Thomas, with sudden exasperation.

As the door closed behind them Josiah paused to mop
his forehead. "Another time, young man, tha'll 'appen
leave me out of thy schemes." Antony grinned at him
sympathetically.

"Any good my apologising? I admit, I didn't fore-
see——"

"Never mind." Akeroyd spoke more briskly, and moved
off across the landing. "I want to see young Stephen."

"I'd like a word with you first, sir." He waved a hand
invitingly. "In my room——" The other looked irritated,
and growled something under his breath; but after a moment
he followed, and allowed himself to be provided with
the best chair and a light for his cigarette.

"Well?" he said. "What have you got to say for
yourself?"

"Only that I'd rather you didn't raise the subject of
those tests with Stephen just yet. I've asked him to keep
what he knows to himself."

"Dammit, Maitland, I've a right to know."

"Yes, of course!" He spoke soothingly, and was conscious for a moment, beneath his worry, of a flash of
amusement at this reaction. Akeroyd roused in him none
of the antagonism he felt for Sir Thomas, though in his

own way he was capable of being equally obstructive. "I want to be sure, you see, that the people who know the results are the ones *I* want informed."

Josiah took his time to digest this, and showed no evidence that he liked what he heard. Antony added, persuasively: "The work has been done, the data is still there to repeat the runs . . . whatever happens to Naylor it will still be available."

That brought Akeroyd up short. He repeated, "Whatever happens to Stephen——?" in a sharp, questioning way. "Do you think the lad's in danger?" he demanded.

" 'appen," said Antony, slipping unconsciously into the other man's idiom. He saw that Akeroyd was not prepared to accept this evasion, and added in a more forthright way: "He will be, when it's known——"

"I see." He sounded discouraged, but did not pursue the subject. "There is also, I suppose, the danger that he may be arrested?"

"That, certainly. Though I think the police will hold their hands until the Ministry make a move." He had been standing by the window, but now he moved to the desk and pushed some papers aside and sat on the corner of it. "It's my responsibility that he's still free," he said; and his sombre tone made the other look at him sharply. "But I don't know if I did right. Guilty or innocent, he'd probably be safer in prison."

Akeroyd did not reply to that directly, but after a pause he said: "I expect he'd rather take the chance, and—even if I thought I could influence you—I should try to respect his decision. That isn't easy, as perhaps you know."

"It isn't easy," Antony agreed. "Not when it's someone you're fond of." And he thought of Jenny's hands twisting together as she listened to George's proposal all those weeks ago in Kempenfeldt Square; and of her quiet voice disclaiming, without heroics, any right or desire to hold him back. But Josiah was following his own ideas.

"Yes, I am fond of young Stephen," he was saying. "Knew his parents . . . grand chap, Ralph Naylor. The mother—well now. She was a singer, walked out on the pair of 'em when the boy was seven years old and went

back to the stage. Said she couldn't stand the country, too
quiet for her, no gaiety. Did well for herself, too, but
Ralph wasn't one to compromise, all or nothing . . . hard
on the girl, but one can see his point. He left Stephen in
school here, and took himself off abroad not long after. I
don't think he's set foot in England more than a couple of
times since then.'' He paused, and eyed his companion
challengingly. ''Not that I believe half of what those
psychologist-fellers say,'' he went on, ''but I've often
thought . . . not good for a boy to be left like that. Seems
to think he can't trust anybody. Daft, of course.''

''Of course,'' echoed Antony. But who could you trust,
in a place where three men had died, and the man or men
responsible had more than murder to answer for? Where
Akeroyd (whom you ought to be able to take at face value)
was talking now for his own reasons, and no knowing
whether his aim was to present Naylor in a sympathetic
context, or to arouse doubts as to his stability. And always
there was the chance of being too clever, of seeing motives
where none existed.

''That was where I came in,'' Josiah went on. ''School
holidays . . . advice, and so forth . . . told him where
to get his training. He's one of the best brains we've got,
you know . . . well, Basil, of course, and Lund; but Lund
has blind spots, for all his reliability.''

''That brings me,'' said Antony, slowly, ''to a question
I've been wanting to ask you. If I asked you which of your
chaps in the Missile Division had a . . . a gift for brilliant
improvisation, who would you say that description fitted
best?''

There was a long pause. ''I should be bound to say,
Basil Vlasov,'' said Akeroyd at last. ''He's a class by
himself, brilliant *and* practical.'' He stopped again, and
seemed to be screwing up his resolution to put the next
question. ''Does that mean you think——?''

''It means I think that description fits the man who
killed Homer and Weston,'' said Antony, bluntly. ''And
Basil had opportunity equal to the others, and perhaps an
even greater incentive.''

''If you're thinking 'blood's thicker than water,' ''

retorted Josiah, with more energy, "his whole family's here . . . well, I think there's an uncle in France, but——"

"Never mind," said Antony. Suddenly the whole situation was intolerable . . . the questions . . . the suspicions. And Jenny liked Basil. "What about Williams?" he asked.

"Evan? Oh, good run-of-the-mill. Ideal for his present job, thorough, conscientious."

"You don't find his—his eccentricity gets in the way at all?"

"Why should it? I'm eccentric myself, come to that, and no one's ever questioned my competence," growled Josiah; but undeniably he made the admission in a boasting spirit. "No, Evan's all right." He got up, suddenly purposeful, and said in a grumbling tone, "Can't stay here gossiping all day. I'll keep my mouth shut, you can rely on that." But he paused in the doorway, and the look he directed over his shoulder was almost pleading. "Clear it up, if you can . . . before it wrecks us all."

'If I can," said Antony. And repeated the phrase, to the empty room, after the door had closed. The words had a desolate sound, and he got up presently and crossed again to the window. But, as on the night Bill Homer died, the fog was closing in.

CHAPTER THIRTEEN

IT WAS THICK by nightfall, and heavier still by the time Antony dragged himself from the fireside after supper to walk round to the Ramseys' again. He was inclined to fuss at leaving Jenny alone (the Amblers were in, but entertaining their own friends); but she had her own anxieties, and paid little enough attention to what he was saying. He went out at last, ruffled; and Jenny opened a book determinedly and read at least three lines before her eyes left the page and sought the fire again, where she could contemplate, without distraction, whatever pictures she chose.

It was about a quarter of an hour later when a tap on the door announced Stephen Naylor's arrival. He said, apologetically: "Antony said he had to go out. He seemed to think you might be lonely."

Jenny was pleased to have company, and said so. "Besides, it seems ages since we saw you, Stephen; except sometimes at supper."

"I've been working late quite often, I expect Antony told you about that." Stephen's sidelong look was the reverse of casual, though probably that was how it was intended. "I meant to try to talk to him to-night, but he said he had to go out."

"Did you want him specially?"

"Well . . . no," he admitted. "We had a talk this morning. I suppose I keep hoping he'll tell me what he thinks, only he never does."

Jenny smiled at him. "That's rather a lot to expect, isn't it? How often do you speak your thoughts perfectly frankly, to anyone?"

"Too often, I expect." His answering grin was half-hearted, and he went on discontentedly: "I'm being unreasonable, I suppose. It's not a thing I usually give much thought to—other people's opinions. But lately——" He broke off, and spread his hands in an uncharacteristically helpless gesture. "Oh, well," he said. "What have you been doing with yourself, Jenny?"

"This and that," said Jenny, suppressing her irritation at a question which is notorious for its ability to strangle conversation. "I went to tea with Beryl, she——"

But Stephen wasn't listening. He said restlessly: "I expect you find it pretty boring——" but didn't seem to know how the sentence should end, and went down on his knees on the hearthrug with an air of relief at finding an occupation, when a lump of coal rolled out of the grate to smoulder on the tiles. He restored it to its place, swept the hearth with an air of concentration, and said abruptly without looking up from his task: "Can I talk to you, Jenny?"

"Of course you can." Her voice was calm as ever, but something in his tone had disturbed her. Jenny had no illusions about herself in the role of *femme fatale,* but neither had she been blind to the admiration in Stephen's eyes, ever since that first evening in London. She had drawn her own conclusions from the fact that he had seemed to avoid her company; and if these were oversimplified (as was perhaps, in the nature of human relationships, inevitable), they were, none the less, near enough the mark.

"Nothing to worry you," he said quickly. "It's only . . . I was wondering——"

"You'd better tell me." If there was resignation behind the words her tone gave no hint of it.

He looked up at her then. "Why did you come here?" he demanded. "Oh yes, I know, we asked you!" he added, seeing her questioning look. "I'll try to tell you what I mean."

"You mean, I suppose, why did Antony agree——?"

"That's it." He sounded eager now. "You see, I never had much time for people, one way and another. Only then we came to your home that night; and our request was outrageous, not a doubt of that. But Antony accepted it. George made light of that, but I saw his expression; and he didn't like it, he hated it like hell. And you didn't like it either, Jenny.''

"No," said Jenny. Her hands tightened together in her lap as he had seen them tighten that evening in Kempenfeldt Square. Stephen put out his own hand to cover them, and then looked up and laughed a little. She hadn't moved, her eyes were friendly as ever, but he sensed her withdrawal.

"You needn't be afraid, Jenny. I'm not going to make love to you. There's a phrase—isn't there?—about having the instincts of a gentleman. I've none of the instincts, I'm afraid . . . but a good many of the inhibitions.''

She said, with dignity: "I wasn't afraid." And he laughed again, and released her hands.

"Of course not," he agreed. And added with sudden violence: "*You* came because you love him—don't you? But I shouldn't ask you that.''

"It doesn't matter," said Jenny. "But of course I do." It was only later that the oddness of their conversation occurred to her; now she looked down at Stephen, and thought only that he needed help. She added gently: "I don't think I can answer your other question, about why Antony agreed to come. I only know he'd despise himself if he hadn't. My part is more simple: I promised myself, long ago when first he went into the Army, that I'd never try to hold him back, whatever he felt he should do . . . however much I wanted to say 'take care,' I'd never say it.'' She stopped there, knowing she had been less than frank, for certainly she had a very good idea of her husband's feelings; but she couldn't say, after all, "he came because he was afraid," even if she thought Stephen's imagination would have carried him to her meaning, past all the inadequacies of words. Jenny herself, who had realised and accepted long ago the fact that no companionship could be complete that did not recognise weakness as well as strength, could remember— with a feeling that was now almost amusement—how bitter that realisation had been to her, when the war was in its early days and she was eighteen years old. But none of that could be spoken, and so she smiled again at Stephen, and said with sudden comprehension: "You know, that's the way it is when people are fond of each other."

Stephen was frowning. "Not always," he said. And then, as though reluctantly: "I think I've only met the deserters."

"Not everyone." She sounded positive. "And, Stephen . . . have you ever given anyone a chance?"

He came to his feet then, and stood looking down at her. She thought he was angry, but after a moment his tension relaxed and he said lamely: "I don't know what you mean."

"Oh, don't be so silly," said Jenny. "Of course you do!"

"Well, I suppose . . . there was a girl," he admitted.

"What happened?"

"Nothing whatever." He grimaced at some private thought. "I told you, I'm not much of a hand at trusting people; and I don't like getting hurt." He looked at Jenny again. "Have you met Susie?" he asked.

"Several times, at the Ramseys'. I don't think you're being very sensible, Stephen." She produced the accusation primly, and saw with pleasure that his expression lightened.

"Perhaps not," he admitted. "I've been wondering lately, Antony may have come here for his own ends, but I've got a feeling I can trust him. And if I can, that rather makes a difference."

"I call that pretty cold-blooded," she said, severely. "And look at it the other way: can Susie trust you?"

Stephen looked startled by this attack, and said uneasily: "I don't know about that."

"Well, I do. Making love to married women——"

"I didn't!"

"If I'd given you the slightest encouragement . . . and then, I suppose, it would have been all my fault. I've no patience with you, Stephen Naylor. You haven't the . . . the guts of a louse!"

He looked at her unbelievingly for a moment, and then—as the contrast became apparent between her air of outraged virtue and the phrase she had so incredibly used—he began to laugh. After a moment her indignation faded, she said: "I mean it, really," but began to laugh as well. They were conversing companionably in the firelit room when Antony came home an hour later.

His own evening had not been a comfortable one. Beryl was at home, and had persuaded her sister-in-law at last to come and stay with her. It wasn't difficult, therefore, to get George on his own, leaving the two women in possession of the sitting-room; but getting him to talk had been another matter. Only it was one thing that could be cleared up, Antony thought, and so it must be done. If he could explain George's attitude, even to his own satisfaction. . . .

It had come out at last, a sorry enough tale; a shabby little secret that would not, perhaps, have proved very worrying to a different sort of man. A wartime romance, a girl who had died in the London bombing while Ramsey was overseas, a child adopted into a comfortable home but still the object of its father's anonymous solicitude. Who else but George could so have bungled matters as to give himself away to his brother-in-law? Who else (as Antony demanded angrily of Jenny when at last they were alone together) who else would have failed to see that one good lie, stoutly adhered to, would have carried him over his difficulties? Nothing easier than to speak of a marriage, Beryl at least would never have doubted his word. But even admitting the worst, how bad was it? How much notice would his family and friends have taken of so ancient a skeleton, how much would his wife really have been hurt? "Quite a lot, perhaps," said Jenny unexpectedly.

"Do you think so?" He was concentrating on his problem, and added seriously: "Put yourself in her place."

Jenny thought: I can't do that. Beryl has a son, so at least she needn't be jealous. But because that was an idea too bitter to share she laughed instead, and told him: "I wouldn't really like being married to George; besides, I'm sure he'd never have asked me."

"I should hope not, indeed," said her husband. But he spoke absently, and was still going over the evening's revelations. "He knew to a penny—damn him!—what I could afford," George had said miserably. And had seemed only a little comforted when it was pointed out to him that his troubles in this respect might now be considered at an end.

"But I can just see Weston gloating over the whole wretched business," said Antony. And he thought as he spoke of Basil Vlasov, who might be hard up because he, too, was paying blackmail. But that was an idea he did not, at present, wish to share. He leaned back in the chair Stephen had vacated and added with an amused look that made Jenny forget, momentarily, how tired he had been when he came in: "I must say," he remarked, "I'd give a deal to know what he had on Sir Thomas. I wonder if we ever shall."

CHAPTER FOURTEEN

GENERAL AIRCRAFT worked a five-day week, though in the case of the Missile Division at least the arrangement seemed to be purely nominal. Both Stephen and Basil went to Carcroft at the usual time next morning, but they went independently and there still seemed to be some disquiet between them. Antony had it on Constable Gill's word that Dick Appleby had not stirred from the house the previous evening; but in spite of what had presumably been an early night he had slept in—this being an indulgence tolerated by Mrs. Ambler on a Saturday, though she would have frowned on it on the Sabbath.

Antony and Jenny went into Mardingley, to call at the library and meet George and Beryl Ramsey for coffee. George's spirits had revived a good deal since the previous evening, though from time to time he seemed to recollect himself and assumed a portentous air as fitting the present circumstances. Beryl, a plump, pretty young woman with a temperament normally phlegmatic, seemed ill at ease. She talked incessantly to Jenny in a low voice, and showed signs, inexplicably, of being affronted when she caught sight of Evan Williams and Linda Carleton eating cream cakes in amiable silence at a nearby table.

Luncheon at Holly Royd was an uncomfortable meal, an unusual state of affairs. Jenny might complain of "shop," but it kept the men busy and reasonably amused; and even Antony—though he could have imagined more exhilarating topics—had sufficient feeling for the job he was doing to give the latest gossip from the works his serious attention. To-day, however, even Basil seemed to have lost some of his normal placidity. He established himself by the fire in the living-room as soon as the meal was over, accompanied by a book with a long and discouraging title; Dick Appleby took himself off with a muttered reference to "turning up the bike"; Jenny was clearing the table; Antony caught Stephen's eye, and jerked his head towards the stairs. When he reached the upper landing the younger man was at his heels.

The fire in the bedroom was not alight, but the room was reasonably warm. Antony shut the door firmly. "Have you any plans?" he asked.

"For to-day? No, I haven't. As a matter of fact," he added, with one of his sudden bursts of candour, "I don't find this business of being followed particularly amusing."

"I'm sorry about that," said the other. "I've an expedition in mind for this evening. The police needn't bother you."

"Well, they do," Stephen retorted. "Still, I'm game. Where do you want to go?"

"To Harrogate," said Antony. "That is, if Appleby makes his usual trip. What time to you suppose he'll leave?"

Stephen frowned. "Not before four o'clock," he said. "You'll have plenty of warning, though; he's mucking about with the motor-bike, so he'll have to come in to change——" He broke off, to voice the question that obviously was uppermost in his mind. "I heard what you said, of course, that night at George's. Does that mean you think——?"

"I think—if you must know—that he is probably a go-between, a subordinate in this business."

"Dick!" said Stephen. "It doesn't seem possible."

"Well, I don't see him as a principal, do you?" demanded Antony, ignoring the obvious trend of the other man's thoughts.

"No, no, of course not. But—look here!—what if he's just visiting a girl-friend? I always thought——"

"Then we shall be wasting our time. What does it matter? It seems likely there will be a message, though . . . an alert, at least."

"It may be more than that." Stephen's tone was urgent.

"I haven't told anybody about the tests, but the data's all there——"

"But not in Appleby's possession." Maitland was positive.

"How do you know that?"

"Your friends the police . . . they have their uses. Between them and Sergeant Billing on the gate——"

"I see. And I haven't brought anything away from the lab either, I suppose they've told you that. Disappointing for you." He spoke with a revival of his former bitterness; and Antony answered him bluntly, but without impatience.

"I've told you, Stephen, I can't afford to gamble on anyone's integrity—least of all on yours."

"Yet you're asking me to help you."

"Certainly." His grin was sympathetic and disarming, and Stephen smiled back reluctantly. "I prefer you under my eye at the moment, for more reasons than one."

"It sounds well . . . put like that."

"In words of one syllable: I don't want you killed. And if anything else happens, it might be helpful to have you with me."

"Was that why you put the police on my tail?"

"It seemed a good idea at the time." He sounded vague, and his tone held no hint of apology. "However . . . this evening. Are you on?"

"Yes, I'll come." He didn't sound eager. Maitland, who was not without sympathy with his obvious distaste for the errand, gave him no further opportunity of withdrawal, but plunged into arrangements. Stephen was in no state to think of mundane matters like a tank full of petrol; and, besides, he wanted an opportunity of consulting with Sergeant Murray, which could not be done on the telephone from Holly Royd.

It was past five o'clock before Appleby set out, which was lucky as it happened, because it was by then quite dark. The problem of keeping him under observation did not, therefore, present too much difficulty; nor was it likely to until they reached the outskirts of the town. Stephen, who was driving the Jaguar, was inclined to hang back, but closed the gap a little in obedience to his companion's directions. One set of headlights looks very like another. Antony was more concerned with their destination; Appleby's Saturday jaunts were reputedly to Harrogate, but after all, they didn't really know he went there. After they had passed Blubberhouses, however, and had ignored the road that led across Snowdon Moor to Otley, taking instead the most direct route towards the spa, he relaxed a little. "But we'll have to look out at Dangerous Corner," he remarked. "He'd turn right there if he was making for Leeds or Bradford. Or he might double back towards Pateley."

Naylor's eyes were on the road ahead. "You seem to know this district well," he said.

"I was here a while in the early days of the war." He spoke shortly, reacting with automatic irritation to a question that invited his thoughts to turn in an unwelcome direction. But a moment later he relented; the remark had, after all, been a casual one, and did not call for a snub. Like Jenny the evening before, he spoke out of sympathy with his companion, in whom he sensed an uncertainty which called for a greater degree of candour than was natural to him; but, undeniably, his intention was mischievous as well as sympathetic when he went on: "I've good cause to remember. The first man I killed, it was in a cottage up on Pock Stones Moor."

Stephen's reaction to his piece of childish display was all that could have been desired. His hands tightened on the steering-wheel, and he shot a brief, startled glance at his companion. After a moment, however, he said evenly enough: "I begin to think that our expedition this evening may be more enlivening that I had supposed." But added, with a spurt of indignation: "Springing a thing like that . . . you might have had us both in the ditch."

"You're driving," the other pointed out. "If it comforts you at all, I'm not expecting trouble."

"Thank you," said Naylor, politely. "I can't tell you how relieved I am." Antony grinned to himself at the pompous tone, and settled himself back again to resume his watch.

Dangerous Corner was passed, and the other possible

turning-point at Four Lane Ends. There was more traffic now, but most of it against them; Dick was taking his time, no doubt it was cold enough to chill any tendency towards excessive speed. Stephen accelerated, and they took the turn by the gas-works close behind the motorcycle; Maitland straightened, intent now on the man they were following. "Keep your eyes for the traffic," he ordered. "I'll direct you."

He wondered later whether they could have managed so well if the route had been a less direct one. Stephen followed instructions docilely enough, but there was no call for any great display of quickness. Even in this after-Christmas period the shops were bright as they went up Parliament Hill. There was a tangle of cars at the top, the late shoppers who had lingered for tea and the advance guard of the evening pleasure seekers. They were so close now that Appleby must have seen them if he had any attention to spare; luckily, he was occupied with his own manœuvers. They followed him, presently, along the broader road towards the Stray, and turned at last, still in his wake. The motor-cycle drew ahead again, slowed finally, and turned into a narrow strip of driveway beside a large, creeper-covered house. "Don't stop, you fool," snapped Maitland. "Drive straight on."

They took the next opportunity of turning, drove back a little way, and left the car. "Ten to one he's calling on his girl," said Stephen. "What'll you bet?"

"Very likely," said Antony placidly.

"Well . . . what then?"

"The game continues. I can ask the police to check up later, but I didn't want to have them dogging his every footstep . . . not yet." He did not add that the police, instead, had *them* in view. Constable Gill was acting with commendable caution, but the knowledge, he felt, would not comfort his companion.

"You've quite made up your mind, haven't you . . . about Dick?"

"That's a dangerous thing to do, but you can take it I'll be surprised if I'm wrong."

"I don't see why——?"

"I don't suppose you do. But why should you be so particularly surprised that I suspect Appleby? If we were following Basil, now, or Evan Williams——?"

"I expect I should feel just as badly," Stephen admitted. "But you said you didn't think Dick was solely responsible. Does that mean . . . someone else in the lab?"

"Some member of the Missile Division . . . or George . . . or Akeroyd," said Maitland. "It's no use being sentimental, Stephen, you may as well face the facts." He saw with satisfaction that this accusation had rendered his companion speechless, and they walked on in silence until they reached the gateway into which Dick Appleby had turned. The motor-cycle was parked unobtrusively at one side of the drive, but there was no sign of its owner. The house was a large one, and almost completely in darkness; only from one tall window to the right of the front door a light gleamed faintly through heavy, brown curtains.

"What now?" asked Stephen softly, as they passed the opening. Antony turned, and began to retrace his steps.

"Number ten," he said, reflectively. "We'd better get back to the car."

The wait that followed tried Stephen's nerves and his patience. He was back in the driver's seat, and for a time he remained alert, ready to start the car at an instant's notice; after a while, however, he reached for his cigarette case, and glanced sidelong at his companion, who still stood beside the car. Maitland's face was impassive, and he showed no sign that he was irked by the delay. After a moment, as though sensing the other man's regard, he turned his head so as to look down at him.

"It's cold, isn't it? Are you sorry you came?"

"No," said Naylor, briefly. And was all at once conscious of the biting chill of the wind, of the quietness of the street, and of the muted sound of traffic from the main road not far away.

A door slammed, and footsteps sounded on gravel; not near, not far away. Maitland stiffened, and turned his head again to listen. After a few moments he said, in a puzzled way. "I thought that was Appleby." And then, more urgently: "Something's up. Stay where you are, Stephen. I'm going to see."

Naylor was at his heels when he reached the gateway of Number Ten, and saw as clearly the events that followed. But in that first instant neither of them realised what had happened. Stephen was conscious only of bewilderment, otherwise his mind was blank of ideas. Antony thought that Appleby was drunk, and wondered—rather impatiently—how he had managed it so quickly. He had a restraining hand on his companion's arm, and was about to counsel retreat, when something in Dick's manner struck him, and he moved forward again, though still cautiously and keeping in the shadow of the hedge.

Appleby was standing beside the motor-cycle, and as they watched he took hold of the handlebars, but slackly; more as though he were seeking support than as if he had any very clear intention about starting the machine. He did not seem to know they were approaching, even when Stephen incautiously left the grass verge, and a little spurt of gravel betrayed the movement. Antony abandoned his caution, and went forward more quickly. He could see now that Dick was breathing with difficulty and that his face was damp with sweat; and—as at last he seemed to realise he was not alone—Appleby looked full at him, and his lips moved as though he were trying to say something. But no words came. His hands unclasped slowly, he took a couple of steps in the direction of the gate, stumbled, and fell heavily. Stephen, moving towards him, was halted by a sharp command. "Leave him!" said Maitland, and fell to swearing under his breath. "I didn't expect *this*," he added over his shoulder, already moving towards the house. "Come on!" But Stephen was kneeling on the gravel beside the fallen man.

The front of the house was dark now, no welcoming porch light, not even the dim glow that had previously been visible. Antony wasted no time there, if someone wanted to leave it was the back way they would take, but ten to one they had gone already.

Dick Appleby lay where he had fallen, and Stephen laid hands on him awkwardly in the darkness. It wasn't until he went to turn him on his back that he discovered the knife. And at the same moment he heard a step on the path behind him, and Constable Gill's voice, as placid as ever. "It's Mr. Naylor, isn't it? Now what's going on?"

By ten o'clock they were back in Mardingley, but were still at the police station. Maitland, who felt he had run the full scale of emotions during the evening, had returned now to the simplest of all of them—he was furiously angry, and had ceased to care who knew it. Under the glare of the old-fashioned, white, shaded bulbs in the sergeant's office his face looked white with fatigue. "I tell you, Murray," he said, for perhaps the tenth time, "Naylor was behind me, and I saw Appleby fall before he ever went near him."

"Yes, Mr. Maitland, we understand that." The policeman's tone was patient, and only faintly weary. "But the fact remains, somebody stabbed him. There was nobody in the house, you saw that for yourself; and the constable on the beat says the occupier left for a holiday trip earlier in the week, and asked him to keep an eye on the place."

"That could be a blind," said Antony, stubbornly. "We saw a light——"

"And Appleby had a key of the front door in his pocket. *That* cock won't fight, Mr. Maitland."

"I suppose not. Who was this occupier, anyway? Oh, I know," he added angrily, "his name was Godolphin, and he had lived there for about six months." He paused, and glared challengingly at the sergeant; but it was Gill who answered, looking up from the report he was composing quietly at a side-table.

"Elderly gentleman, thought to be retired. One general servant, who had already gone on holiday, or so he told Constable Myers. Does that help you, sir?"

"No," snapped Maitland, and resumed his pacing of the room. Gill laid down his pen, and began to tidy his papers. Stephen, almost forgotten as the argument raged round him, looked across frowningly and said in his abrupt way:

"You're wasting time, Antony. If the sergeant here has made up his mind——"

"Well, Mr. Naylor, it's like I told you. On the evidence as it stands I've no alternative but to detain you. When we have the medical report, now——"

"And when the house has been gone through," put in Antony.

"That, of course. But there were no bloodstains," Murray pointed out.

"With the knife in the wound there couldn't have been more than a trace. You may find something," Antony insisted.

Later, when Gill and Stephen had left them, he was still standing in the middle of the room, making no move to go. Murray said patiently: "We'll not do any good, going over it all again to-night, Mr. Maitland," and he came to himself with a start, and laughed without amusement.

"That's true enough. I seem to have been wrong all along the line. I took Stephen with me because I thought *he* was in danger; and if anything happened to Appleby, I thought it would be here, or at the works. I thought it would look like an accident." He broke off, and for the first time looked at the policeman with a sort of apology. "I can see your point, you know," he admitted.

"That," said Murray dryly, "has been only too obvious. But I don't quite understand——"

"I want things brought to a head." He was impatient again. "If Naylor's guilty, you'd never prove it as things stand now. And if he's being framed, the chap I'm looking for may have sufficient restraint to keep quiet for a while, rather than spoil his effect. Unless I can think of something——"

"I hope you will." Murray's tone was polite, but not encouraging. His mind seemed to be elsewhere, and he added after a pause: "I had the impression your concern for Mr. Naylor was more personal, like."

"I feel responsible," said Maitland shortly. "He may be safer in jail, I grant you that."

"Then——?"

"Oh, good lord! To ask a man to risk his life . . . that's

bad, I suppose. But to take away his liberty . . . unbear-
able . . . unthinkable!''

"I see, sir," said Murray, carefully; and his companion
laughed again.

"I don't suppose you do. However . . . I'll leave the
car, Sergeant. Ambler can bring it back when he comes
down with a suitcase for Stephen. Is that all right with
you?''

"Perfectly all right, Mr. Maitland.'' Murray was conscious of relief as the door closed softly behind his visitor;
but his frown was puzzled as he walked across to pick up
Gill's report, and he stood fingering the sheets for some
time before he carried them back to his own desk and sat
down to read.

CARGILL'S MOON 141

mping sense of futile inutility. They rocked
of the, like without either of them suffering in

CHAPTER FIFTEEN

THE FIRST THING of note to be recorded of the following day was the unexpected energy of Basil Vlasov, who, finding Antony rummaging in a harassed way through the hall cupboard for gloves and a muffler, offered his company if he were going walking. He was glad enough to have a companion, but added: "I'm going on the moors." Basil laughed at the note of warning.

"I don't mind expending my energies in a worthy cause," he explained. "And I like the country hereabouts. You may be glad of a guide." He glanced towards the staircase. "Is Jenny coming?"

"She said she'd stay with Mrs. Ambler." He added, as he pulled the front door shut behind him: "The old girl's upset, though she'd never admit it."

"Yes. I noticed a certain tendency in her this morning to regard me as a ewe lamb," said Basil pensively. "I don't know quite what role she has cast me for, though," he added, and glanced at his companion, as though hoping to surprise a change of expression.

Their way led them from the residential district, through some meaner streets of terraced houses, past the small community of farms which huddled at the foot of Cargill, and up the steep road towards the moor. Presently they turned on to one of the tracks that led away, still climbing, to the right. Basil, without any appearance of haste, fell into a swinging stride that matched his companion's. It was a bright day, clear and very cold; they went in silence for the most part, and it was not very long before Antony's dejection left him. He could not, if challenged, have claimed to be feeling precisely happy; but he felt alive again, and the cramping sense of inertia had left him. They reached the top of the rise without either of them suffering the ignominy of losing his breath, and struck out across the moor.

They had been walking for almost two hours when Basil slowed his pace, and seemed to be looking for a landmark. After a while he took, determinedly, a turn to the left; the track was wider here, and ran beside one of the precarious-looking dry stone walls that are so common on the moors, and that rarely seem to have any justification for their existence. But a little farther on a stone cottage cowered behind a straggle of wind-distorted larches; it was empty now, and you could only guess where the intake had been, for the moor had long since reclaimed its own.

A quarter of a mile beyond the cottage the track ran out on to rocky ground, there was a sharp drop before them, Basil came to a stop abruptly, and said "There!" with a proprietorial gesture. "I thought you might like to see the view from here," he added, with another of his sidelong glances. "All the kingdoms of the earth, and the glory thereof!"

The view was certainly extensive. Mile upon mile of rolling ground, yellow-brown in the sunshine; with patches of a darker colour, which showed where the ling would blaze in summer. There was also, perhaps a mile distant, and considerably below them, the main road to Pateley Bridge; and beside it—and it was this to which Antony supposed his attention was being directed—the spread of buildings that formed the Carcroft works.

"Looks like a toy from here, doesn't it?" said Basil; but Antony shook his head.

"Far too like a concentration camp," he maintained; and added, thoughtfully: "I was surprised to find that the likeness doesn't persist on closer acquaintance. I was sadly ignorant of everything pertaining to industry, before I came here."

"Including technical matters?" Basil suggested.

"Technical matters in particular," Antony agreed, and perched himself on a convenient boulder. They were reaching, it seemed, the point of the expedition; but the other man was quite capable of finding words for what he had to say, without encouragement. He drew up his heels, clasped his hands round his knees, and settled himself to wait.

Basil was in no hurry to begin. He succeeded in lighting a cigarette in the lee of the wall, and came back to stand leaning against one of the rocks. "I think perhaps I can help you," he said at last. "I ought to say," he added carefully, "that I don't expect you to trust me; but somebody should explain how the project stands, and you can always check up on what I tell you."

"I shall be grateful," said Antony. His tone was noncommittal, and the other man grinned.

"I bet you will," he said. "However. Was I right to infer from Stephen's manner that the results of the last runs he did were satisfactory?"

Maitland turned his head, and gave him a considering look. "Quite right," he said at last. And added, still reflectively: "He said he thought you'd have a good idea——"

"Then I think you should appreciate the position that arises. I had a fair idea what he'd find, though of course you can never be sure of these things. Stephen may have imagined he was maintaining a poker-face, but there can't be anyone in the lab now who isn't pretty certain of it too."

"I shouldn't think so."

"There are, of course, a good many questions I should like to ask," said Basil, "if I thought there was any hope of your answering them. But one I must put to you: is suspicion narrowed down now to someone in the Missile Division?"

"It always seemed most likely, and since Weston's death I should say it was certain; with the two exceptions you know of, Akeroyd and George."

"Then I must explain to you a little more about 'Full Moon.' When the project started there were two distinct lines of approach; our work in the lab—and I expect you have a fair idea about that—and also the metallurgical development and some work on a solid fuel."

"I thought that was one of those things that couldn't be done," said Antony.

"Well, it was, but now it isn't," said Basil, with an air of great clarity. "Anyway, we all started out merrily and independently. The physicists and chemists were in that separate compound, away from the rest of the buildings . . . do you see it? A wire fence like ours, but lots of separate huts."

Antony looked down, to study the works in detail, and after a moment nodded. "Pretty well segregated," he commented. "Explosives?"

"Yes. Altogether too jumpy a job for my taste, I like a quiet life. Anyway, as you can see, there's no direct access from their part to ours, and a pass to Missiles wouldn't necessarily take you in there."

"I knew that, of course," said Antony slowly. "But I didn't realise there was a connection."

"Well, you see, when they had completed the development of the formula, we found that greatly increased speeds were going to be possible, over what we'd allowed for. In particular, we had a problem with stability and roll . . . the damn' thing was spinning round on its longitudinal axis, and the guidance and control system was all to hell. And that, as you can imagine, meant an extensive programme of modifications." Basil paused, and looked at his companion inquiringly; but as the other man made no comment he went on after a moment: "During the past year we've been on that tack, and then—as you know—there was this security scare. Even with the tightened regulations, though, I see no reason to suppose that all the data available hasn't been taken out gradually. At least, that is what I'd do if I were an enemy agent, and they weren't very particular about people taking things out . . . not until after Carleton was killed."

"I appreciate your desire to be helpful," said Maitland with sudden tartness, "but it seems to me you're saying the game's played already, and we've lost."

"Jumping to conclusions—and you a lawyer," remarked Basil reprovingly. He encountered a glare from his companion, and went on soothingly, "I said, that's what I'd do if I were an enemy agent; *but* I wouldn't hand the stuff over piecemeal, I'd wait until I was sure of the completed picture.''

''You say he is sure . . . now.''

''Most likely. But that's where the fuel comes in. Don't you see . . . the whole thing's useless without the formula for that.''

''I see. And if *you* were an enemy agent, how would you set about getting hold of it?''

''That would depend on the degree of urgency. I mean, for a chap in Missiles there's bound to be an opportunity sooner or later—if Josiah called a full meeting, for instance, or he might be persuaded to put some further, independent testing in hand concerning the expected performance.'' He shrugged his shoulders, and glanced up at his companion. ''What effect will Stephen's arrest have?'' he asked. ''And what will happen to him, do you think?''

''I think he'll be sent for trial on the charge of killing Dick Appleby; and I think he'll be acquitted. But meanwhile, the Press will have a field day, skating on—and over—the line of criminal libel. They'll stir up enough mud to ruin him . . . that's what I *think*.'' He shivered as he spoke, and added brusquely: ''It's getting cold, shall we get on?'' And slid down from his rock as Basil nodded.

''But you didn't answer my other question,'' he reminded Antony, as they retraced their steps down the track to the cottage.

''The effect of his arrest . . . on the firm, do you mean? If all is quiet for a while, the Ministry will probably decide he was, in fact, responsible for what has happened, and give the word to continue.''

''That would be X's best bet them . . . to lie low?''

''Undoubtedly.''

''It would lessen your chances of identifying him . . . or have you done that already?''

Antony did not answer immediately. He was looking straight ahead of him, and his expression was sombre; but after they had walked in silence for a while he said slowly: ''I've no proof . . . I may well be wrong. Only a rather doubtful idea about character, and the fact that he lied as

to where he was on one occasion. And as to the first"—he
could not resist a glance at his companion to see how this
was received—"Josiah thought my description of the man
I want applied to you."

"Did he now?" said Basil. "Er—it makes you think,
doesn't it?" He thought for a moment. "You don't sound
very sure," he went on, at last. "Stephen, for instance;
you think he's innocent?"

"Of killing Appleby? I'm sure of it. For the rest . . . he
could be innocent of that, and still responsible——"

"What happened last night?" Basil seemed to have
forgotten his previous resolve to ask no questions.

"Dick went, I suppose, to a house he made a habit of
visiting. The occupier had left; my version is that he found
one of his colleagues waiting for him. He was stabbed,
you know, and left for dead—again, that's what I think.
Later he came to himself, and tried to leave——"

"Is that medically possible?"

"There have been cases. I'm sure of one thing, he was
already sick when we came on the scene. But the police
think he found the house empty, took one drink too many—
he'd certainly had at least one whisky—and collapsed from
the effect. After that, Stephen improved the shining hour
by sticking a knife into him. *Voilà tout!*"

"It is never helpful," remarked Basil, at his most de-
ceptively casual, "to blame oneself for something that
couldn't be avoided."

"It was an error I should have foreseen. However, as
you say, that doesn't help matters now. What do you
suggest?"

"If you want action, it's fairly simple. Get Josiah to
announce the closing of the contract, and call for all the
paper-work to be handed in to his office. Say it's going to
be turned over next day to the Ministry people. The stuff
would be in the vault overnight, of course; but I can't
believe a chap who has got away with so much already
isn't supplied with a set of duplicate keys. A last chance
like that ought to bring X up to scratch, if anything will."
He saw the look of doubt in his companion's face, and
added gently: "I will make you a present of the fact,

which I see is already in your mind: that if I were an enemy agent this is precisely the advice I should give you.''

Antony laughed at that. "If a trap is set, there will be guards, of course."

"The formula will still be more accessible than shut away in the chemistry lab," Basil maintained. "Besides, if one is forewarned, guards can always be . . . taken care of."

"There is also the possibility," the other man objected, "that Josiah is X." He was ignoring the double shock of Vlasov's words, to his nerves, and to his memory. No time now for brooding on the past, a plan must be made and would obviously have its dangers. From what he had seen, he was not inclined to rate the security of the Fuel Research enclosure as highly as his companion seemed to do. That it had not been violated was due, he thought, to the secrecy which had so far been possible. A deadline, such as Basil suggested, would probably bring action; but who was to say in what direction the move would be made? If the matter could be finished . . . "We'll have to take a chance," he said. "It may not work, of course." He turned his head, and encountered squarely Basil's questioning look. "I think he's mad," he said. "So I doubt if he'll count the cost."

"Then you do know," said Basil, bluntly. But there was no answer to that. They came down from the moor in a silence that was no longer companionable.

It seemed to be taken for granted that they should pass the gate of Holly Royd, and make for George's home. The dusk was deepening now, and the lights of the town were welcoming, friendly. Antony had to shake off deliberately the feeling of normality; he had the impression that Basil accepted much more easily than he did the facts that they both knew . . . that some familiar friend was a killer, and worse . . . that this man was both desperate and determined, and that the danger he would succeed was very real.

As they came into the road where the Ramseys' house

stood, Maitland slowed his stride a little. "I suppose we're likely to find a crowd?" he asked. "To-day of all days," said Basil with only the faintest trace of sarcasm in his voice, "I should think it certain." And a moment later he added, "Look."

Antony stopped. Pulled into the drive in front of the closed doors of the garage was Tom Burns's battered MG; and parked in the road, Evan Williams's big Armstrong fronted John Lund's Land-Rover. "That being so," he said reflectively, "a little advance publicity wouldn't do any harm. Will you help me?"

"Willingly," said Basil. He did not elaborate, or ask any further questions; and Antony was glad to let the matter rest at that.

George's welcome was subdued; Beryl said anxiously, "How is Stephen?" but did not seem to expect an answer.

At first glance the sitting-room seemed full of people; Beryl went away to make fresh tea, and Antony made for the fire and took his time to confirm what the cars had told him. Tom Burns and Mickey, side by side on the sofa; John Lund, his chair pulled back, away from the fire; Evan Williams, who—strangely—was the only one to give them a conventional greeting, and who moved from his chair near the hearth to offer it to Basil.

There could, of course, be only one topic of conversation. "This is a ghastly business, Maitland," said John abruptly. "I find it difficult to believe——"

"Dick is dead; there is no doubt of that, at least," said Evan. "Is the rest true, Maitland . . . that Stephen is under arrest?"

"Quite true." He stood with his back to the fire, and surveyed the little group. "Are you sorry . . . all of you?" he added, deliberately.

There was a chorus of protests, with Mickey's voice rising indignantly above the rest. "Stephen wouldn't!" she said. Tom Burns, beside her, gave her a grateful look, and echoed "Of course not!"

Basil, who already looked in danger of falling asleep in the warm room, opened his eyes for a disconcerting moment. "That doesn't come come well from you, Tom."

The young man flushed. "I know I thought . . . but then he told me——" He stammered a little over the words, too anxious to be believed. "Anyway, Basil, he said you were being cagey." Vlasov leaned back, and closed his eyes again.

"A common-sense precaution," he murmured. Burns looked furious for a moment, and then turned back to the girl.

"Oh, what's the use," he muttered. Lund interrupted with his air of quiet authority.

"What we think doesn't matter, after all." He looked across at Maitland and framed his question with care. "Are you . . . will the authorities be satisfied now?"

"On one score . . . yes, most likely. If you're anxious about your project, though, I'm afraid I can't reassure you. Although I've informed the Ministry that there is now no need, they've decided it should be suspended. I imagine that's a prelude to cancellation."

"But they can't do that!" Williams's tone was almost a wail. "It's too important. They can't do it," he repeated. And then he added, with an air of uncertainty: "When you said 'there's no need,' did you mean . . . Stephen?"

"No," said Antony. He looked round the circle of faces and as he caught Basil's eye the thought crossed his mind that the other was looking startled now . . . almost frightened, if that hadn't seemed to unlikely. Unexpectedly, Mickey's eyes had filled with tears; Burns looked mutinous, as though this were something personally directed; George—perhaps less intimately concerned than any of them—had joined Beryl by the tea-tray, but his hand shook a little as he lifted a cup to carry it across the room; Lund said quietly: "In the circumstances it seems . . . but it may be the best thing——" But he did not speak with any conviction.

Basil, in his usual indolent manner, took up the tale. "Josiah told me——" If Antony's impression of a moment before was correct, his manner now gave no hint of it. He made his point well, and none of the men listening could be in any doubt where the vital formula would be the following night . . . nor could they fail to realise that time was running out, that opportunity would not exist much longer. But there was still the coming night to get through; he wondered if Basil realised this, and rather thought he did.

Beryl had gone quietly out of the room, and now came back to catch Antony's eye. "Jenny phoned," she told him. "She wondered if you might be here. Mr. Akeroyd has been trying to get in touch with you . . . it's important he says."

That broke up the party. Evan Williams spoke of "being expected"; Lund remembered that Johnny would be home by now; George said quietly, "I'll drive you, Antony." And added, with a fair attempt at a normal manner, "You too, Basil; you must be exhausted." Only Tom Burns and Mickey remained; they had probably, Antony reflected, nowhere half so comfortable to go.

Akeroyd, who was a widower, lived at a private hotel near the centre of Mardingley. Antony put through a call to Holly Royd from the telephone box at the corner, and was relieved when, after only a slight delay, he heard Jenny's voice.

"Everything under control, love?"

"Oh, yes. Susie's with me." To his ears, the note of strain was very evident; there was a gentle serenity about Jenny that invited confidences, but she was ill-equipped for bearing other people's unhappiness. "Did you get my message?" she added.

"Yes, I'm just going to see him now. Only I wanted to know——"

"Mr. and Mrs. Ambler are going to Chapel in a few minutes, but Susie says she'll stay. Don't fuss, darling."

"All right, I'll try not to be long." He rang off, and stood for a moment thinking, before he went out into the cold street again to walk the few steps to the dimly lighted entrance to the Devonshire Hotel.

Josiah's room was comfortably overcrowded with old-fashioned furniture, and a good deal too warm for his visitor's taste. His accent was very marked this evening, and it was obvious that he was deeply disturbed.

"I'm glad to see thee, lad, and that's a fact. It may be nowt, when all's said, but—"

"What's happened, sir?"

"I had a call from the works police. The chap on duty to-night in the Fuel Research enclosure noticed some strands of cloth caught in the wire at the top of the fence. Looked as if they came from a Burberry." He looked inquiringly at his companion, as though anxious to see how this struck him. "Summat and nowt, most likely," he said. "*Could* anybody get over?"

"There are ways," said Antony slowly. He stood very still for a moment, while the cold realisation of failure swept over him. Too late now for the trap he had placed such hopes in; too late even to stop 'Full Moon' from being presented, in detail, to men well qualified to make use of this new knowledge. Too late . . . or was it? He looked at Josiah, and said as though with an effort: "The new fuel?"

"The formula and process sheets were locked away. I've sent Fergusson up to check, of course . . . but there was no sign, only the scrap of cloth."

"I see." More than enough . . . more than enough . . . he tore his mind from the useless repetition. "You realise, I suppose, that this vital information——?"

Akeroyd looked suddenly an old man. "I should have made it clear to you," he said. "I didn't realise, I suppose, how little a casual reference would mean to anyone like yourself. And there was nothing wrong, except in Missiles——" (And who can I blame for the omission, thought Antony . . . except myself?)

Too late to worry now. He said, speaking his thoughts aloud: "This means a break, I think . . . that he means to leave the country. Straight from killing Appleby, I should have realised——"

Josiah came a step closer. "Who?" he asked; but Antony ignored the question, or at least his answer was an indirect one.

"Ring the police for me," he said. "Tell them I've gone to Lund's house. Ring the local security people—I'm writing down the number. Tell them this means he must have made plans for a get-away, but he was still in Mardingley half an hour ago.''

"John Lund?'' Akeroyd echoed the name stupidly. Maitland picked up the phone, and moved it across the table towards him, before going swiftly out of the stuffy room. There was a cab rank opposite the station; the house was high on the moor road, half-way up Cargill, but he could be there, with luck, in twenty minutes. He did not stop to consider the chances of success, failure seemed only too likely. But John wouldn't leave the boy, and that might have delayed him. Characteristically, he acted now without hesitation; but the risks were clear in his mind and he accepted them coldly.

He could have waited for the police, of course, if only the time element hadn't become so important. But he didn't want to live with himself afterwards . . . if he waited and then they were too late.

CHAPTER SIXTEEN

THE HOUSE was long and low, with a cluster of buildings at the rear to show that once, at least, it had been a farmer's. As the old taxi chugged its way down the hill, it left behind a silence that was complete and menacing. Antony, turning up his collar against the increasing cold, pushed open a gate that creaked, he thought, like a gate in a radio play (the sound effect that conveys to intelligent listeners the authentic atmosphere of a lonely moor; just as the endless cry of seagulls is all that is needed to suggest a coastal scene). The flagged path was uneven under his feet, and when he reached the porch he could hear, faintly from the back of the house, the sound of lusty hymn-singing. The housekeeper was home, it seemed, and enjoying Sunday evening in her own way with the wireless turned well up. There was no light on above the door, and none showed from the front windows. He pushed the bell, and waited.

There was a pause. He began to wonder whether an attack on the knocker might have more success, when the door swung open suddenly, startling him because he had heard no footsteps approaching. The room within was lamplit, but it seemed very bright after the darkness outside. Johnny Lund was backing away from the door; just for an instant there no mistaking the fact that he looked frightened. Then he made an obvious effort to get a grip on his emotions.

"I only just put the phone down. You couldn't know I called."

"Did you want me, Johnny?" Maitland stepped into the room, and pushed the door shut behind him. He had a wary eye lifting for his surroundings, but for the moment at least they seemed to be alone, and it was obvious that the boy was in need of reassurance.

"Yes, I . . . well I thought, perhaps——" He was standing his ground now, but he did not look at the newcomer. Antony ignored his obvious distress and asked bracingly:

"Is your father in? I wanted to see him."

"He . . . no, he came in for a few minutes. But he isn't here now." He broke off, and—as though unwillingly—his eyes met Antony's.

"What's the matter, Johnny?" His tone was gentle now, and he stood very still near the door; feeling instinctively that any movement would be as startling to the boy as to a wild or nervous animal. "I'd like to help," he said.

"I don't know . . . truly, I don't know, Mr. Maitland. I . . . I think he's ill."

"May I come in, then?" He ignored the evasion, walked across to the fire and kicked it to a blaze. When it was burning to his liking he stretched his hands towards it, and turned to smile at Johnny Lund. "It's cold, isn't it? Come to the fire, you look as if you need to get warm."

Johnny came reluctantly, his eyes wary. "Now then, tell me," the visitor commanded.

"It's nothing, sir . . . nothing, really!" His voice rose a little on the protest. "Just a thought I had——"

Antony judged it time to have done. "Dammit, don't lie to me!" he snapped (and heard with distaste, even in that moment of strain, the echo in his voice of a schoolmaster he had detested long ago). Johnny stiffened, and said with a queer sort of dignity:

"I *wasn't* lying. Only, it isn't easy——"

"Of course it isn't," agreed the other, and smiled again. Johnny came slowly towards him, and stood in the circle of firelight, and rubbed his forehead in a worried way.

"He seemed strange, ever since I got home for the holidays," he confided. "One thing, he always seemed to talk as if I wouldn't be going back to school again; but when I asked him he . . . wasn't very pleased . . . he said I was imagining things. He always talks a lot about what I'm going to do when I leave school, so that was nothing new. Of course, he was worried about what was happening at the works, but who wouldn't be? He didn't tell me much about it, only there's always talk, you know.'' He stopped, but his eyes were steady now on his companion's face. "I'm trusting you, Mr. Maitland,'' he said sadly. "I don't know what else to do.''

Antony made no reply. A younger boy he might have tried to comfort; an older one might have been ready for a rational explanation of what was happening; Johnny Lund, at fifteen, had left the magic circle of childhood without having attained, as yet, any of the protective covering of the adult. So the man waited, but the boy's next words almost jarred him out of his deliberate calm.

"To-night, when I saw what was in his brief-case, I knew I must do something. Rolls and rolls of microfilm——''

"You didn't touch them?'' He could not contain the question, though he heard with self-directed anger the strain in his voice that might well startle the boy out of making further confidences. Strangely, the effect seemed to be quite the opposite.

"If you mean, did I expose them, of course I didn't.'' Johnny sounded scornful. "But I thought perhaps someone had put them there, to—to incriminate him, you know. Because, of course, I've heard talk——'' He paused, to see how his companion was taking this, but Antony said only:

"What did you do with them?''

"Oh, I left them there. But I thought I ought to tell Dad about them. So when he came in——'' Again his look changed, the momentary confidence was gone, he put up a hand to push back his hair and said in a voice that had taken on a higher pitch: "Why do you make me tell you? You know—don't you?—what I'm going to say.''

"You'd better tell me it all,'' said Antony. And again he waited. In face of what he knew, there was nothing to be done for Johnny, except to end the nightmare as quickly as might be. That he needed the boy's help was unfortunate, but he couldn't afford to be squeamish about accepting it. If Lund had gone already . . .

"He said he'd given me enough time.'' Johnny's voice

was low now, and controlled. "He said he hadn't meant to make a move just yet, but things were happening too quickly. He said we were going away. I didn't understand it all, sir; he wasn't being very . . . very lucid. But he talked about 'unlimited opportunities,' and people who were too stupid to understand the importance of science's contribution——"

"Don't worry about all that, Johnny, I think I know. You didn't go with him, after all?"

"He's gone up to the lab, I think. He said he'd be about an hour, and I was to pack for both of us while he was gone." He looked up at his companion, his feeling of bewilderment only too obvious. "I didn't know what I *ought* to do," he said. "I don't want to go away, of course . . . to leave England; but that wasn't why I didn't do as he said. I telephoned you instead, but then when you came in I didn't know . . . I wished I hadn't." He was near tears now, and Antony put out a hand and gripped his shoulder.

"You did the right thing, Johnny, don't ever doubt that. I can't promise you a happy ending, you know, I think your father is ill . . . very ill. But you've plenty of friends, they won't let you down." He dropped his hand, and added more briskly: "Now! Do you know why he went to the lab?"

"He said there was something he wanted to photograph . . . microfilm, I expect."

"I see." The final touch, the details of the fuel? The papers that had been stolen might well be too bulky for convenient transportation. "Did he . . . did he take his brief-case with him?" And again he was trying to keep the eagerness from his tone.

"It's over there," said Johnny. His casual manner was mimicry, perhaps; but just for the moment he was master of himself. He nodded his head towards the corner by the door, and went on—perhaps because silence, just then, was something to be afraid of: "It's pretty shabby, isn't it? I remember Mother once wanted to give him a new one, but he said——"

Maitland had his hand on the case when he heard the car

draw up, and took a firmer grip on it as he backed silently
into a position from which he could cover the front door.
Johnny had run to the window, and pulled aside the heavy
curtain. He said in a puzzled way: "It's a car that came up
the hill, not from the works. And there's a lady . . . would
it be Mrs. Maitland, do you think?"

"If you spoke to her on the phone," said Antony,
crossing the room quickly and yanking the door wide, "I
should think it very likely." But the grimness faded from
his expression as his wife came out of the darkness into the
circle of lamplight. She had thrown a coat on, but seemed
not to have stopped to find gloves or a scarf; her cheeks
were flushed, and her hair was blown about wildly. When
she started, a little breathlessly, to explain her presence, he
interrupted her without ceremony.

"I haven't time for explanations, love. Take the boy
with you . . . and go."

No time for explanations . . . no questions, then. Just
for an instant Jenny looked at him, and then she turned and
smiled at Johnny. "Will you come with me, I'd be glad of
your company." The boy moved towards her; the evening
seemed to have taken on a dream-like quality, but he could
not have told whether his obedience was due to her encouragement, or to the man's urgent tone. But before they
reached the door it was pushed wider open, and John Lund
came in.

Antony was back in his chosen position; he had the
doorway covered, but Jenny—about to leave—was between
him and the newcomer. Lund, who seemed to have taken in
the situation with startling speed (but, of course, he must
have been warned by sight of the Jaguar, parked outside),
took one step into the room and grabbed Jenny round the
waist. Thus shielded, he retreated again, pulling her with
him, until he could kick the door shut behind him.

"A cold night," he remarked pleasantly. And added
with a politeness that was grotesque in its unreality: "It
was good of you to come out, this weather." Across
Jenny's brown curls his eyes mocked the man who was
now his enemy.

Johnny said: "Dad——" but the man snapped "Be

quiet!'' at him, without turning his head. To Maitland, his voice had still its customary amiability. "I didn't expect you yet, though I felt to-night that you guessed . . . something. Why did you bring Mrs. Maitland?''

"I wanted her to take the boy away,'' said Antony, with truth. Jenny twisted a little, to look back at him over her shoulder. He saw, with amazement, that her eyes were as steady as ever. He pushed down the sick feeling of fear and said, deliberately casual: "If I give you my gun, will you let them go?''

Lund seemed to consider. "I think not,'' he said at length. "I could, however—er—unhand your wife. That would be something to the good, wouldn't it?'' He nodded towards the round, pedestal table that stood between them. "If you put it there——''

"If I don't——?'' said Antony. And was taken unawares by the sudden malignancy of Lund's expression. "All right,'' he said. The exchange was effected. Lund, with the gun in his hand, unclasped his arm from Jenny's waist and pushed her aside. She moved across to the hearth-rug to stand beside Johnny, and half expected a curt command to stop. But Lund's attention was fixed again on the other man. "There is also my brief-case,'' he suggested.

"I wondered when we should get to that.'' Antony spoke slowly, and moved a pace or two nearer the table, and paused again, as if irresolute. He was under no illusions as to the danger of the situation: mad or not, Lund had killed and killed again to serve his purpose. He had thought once "a thing like that might well be worth a man's life''; now he could fix his mind on "Full Moon'' only with an effort. Some cold sense of logic told him that he must do what he could, that this was important, vital; but every human emotion clamoured that he should seek a way to safety—was there such a way? If he died, Jenny would die too. But he took his decision coldly at last, and the others had no time to become aware of his agony of indecision. He stood by the table and kept his hands on the brief-case, and looked at Lund with derision.

"I'm afraid you'll be disappointed,'' he said, and saw the sudden alarm in the other man's eyes. "Didn't you notice how bright the fire is," he added, tauntingly. "Microfilm makes a good blaze." And just for the moment he needed Lund's eyes wavered, and sought the hearth. In the same instant he received the brief-case full in his face; and felt, as he staggered back, a grip on his wrist that was too painful to be argued with. As he straightened himself, he saw Maitland back in his old place at the other side of the table, in the act of transferring the gun from his left hand to his right. He said a little breathlessly:

"Was that true . . . or just a trick?"

Antony smiled at him vaguely. He was not just then in any case to give a considered answer, having wrenched his shoulder in the scuffle and being mainly concerned to overcome the feeling of nausea that this had brought on. In the pause, Lund answered his own question. "True?" he said; and sat down heavily on the sofa behind him, kicking pettishly at the brief-case which now lay on the floor at his feet.

"There is still," said Antony, "the formula for the fuel." His voice sounded, ridiculously, in his own ears, as if he were attempting consolation. "I should like that too," he added, more firmly.

"You have the gun," Lund pointed out, and his look was suddenly malicious; it said, as clear as words: 'will you shoot me, with my son looking on?'

Maitland's lips were a thin line. He said, as though the other had spoken his thought aloud: "The boy must take his chance." And added, as Lund's look became complacent: "But I can afford to wait."

"It seems a pity," said John Lund. And all at once, the veneer began to crack. "A bit casual, aren't you?" he said fretfully, "to invite your friends here; without so much as a by-your-leave, as my grandmother used to say."

"I'm sorry," said Antony.

"And I didn't think you'd move till your ridiculous trap was sprung," Lund went on, in a grumbling tone. "How did you know?" he challenged.

"In the last analysis, I was looking for a fanatic. Sir Thomas was sufficiently egotistical, but I did not think his demon would be served by these particular crimes. And your price, Basil told me, would be 'unlimited opportunity.' That made me wonder, and when I heard about the 'Grass Snake' project——''

"That's right! That was what did it! The fools didn't know a good thing when they saw it. The money didn't matter . . . the men didn't matter . . . you can always find more! So I made up my mind, the next time, the information should go where it would be most appreciated." He stopped, and his excitement faded. "I suppose you think I'm mad," he asked. "Because I killed them——''

"I wonder," said Maitland. "And I don't think you killed Carleton," he amended.

"No, you're right there. But I had no choice in the matter, you know, no choice at all. Bill had been a good source of information . . . no reason why he shouldn't talk to me, of course; but when he began to look at me oddly I knew he had to go. I'd forgotten it was so easy."

To the man who was listening, that last casual phrase had more of horror in it than all that had gone before. He closed his lips firmly on a question, but saw with dismay that the subject was to be aired, even without his prompting. Lund turned and looked at his son, and Johnny said—but as though the words were spoken against his will—"Who . . . before?"

"Didn't you guess?" He seemed to lose interest in the boy, and looked again at Maitland, and again there was that appearance of complacency. "She would have spoiled him," he said. "Always saying I drove him too hard. But Johnny has brains, I couldn't let her interfere. So when she was ill——'' He paused, and looked from one to other of his listeners with that ill-concealed air of self-satisfaction. "It only needed patience," he added triumphantly. "Sooner of later the chance is bound to come . . . if you want to kill your wife."

Jenny had an arm round Johnny's shoulders, and after a moment of horrified incomprehension the boy turned and hid his face against her. And it was then they noticed for the first time the sound of a car, grinding up the long hill. But John Lund, enlarging on his theme, seemed merely gratified that his audience was to be augmented; and was still talking five minutes later when the police took him away.

ERROR ON TOPSOL'N 181

...H prickle the rambling paths of Hand's footpath...
O lv... ...ckroned Antony were oppressed at least...

CHAPTER SEVENTEEN

IT WAS THREE DAYS later when Maitland went up to Carcroft works again, for the last time. Stephen drove him, and dropped him at the door of the old house as he had done so often before; this morning it was the younger man who seemed reluctant, and who hesitated before he drove on towards the car-park. But Antony was conscious of his own disinclination, and was glad that Ambler was occupied with a visitor so that there was no need to pause on his way through the hall.

Managing Director and Company Secretary awaited him in the former's office. It was a grey day, with no sunshine to blind him; and he was conscious at once of Sir Thomas's grave look, and the fact that Knowles seemed nervous. It was the latter who voiced the request, breaking an awkward silence that had followed the briefest of greetings.

"I hope, dear boy, that you're going to tell us——"

Antony smiled, amused and set at ease by the familiar form of address. "I came to give you my report," he said, hopefully, and pulled it out of his pocket. And was aware at once of Knowles's downcast look, and of Sir Thomas's gaze fixed almost hungrily on the envelope he had put down on the desk. After a moment, though, he raised his eyes and asked with an air of indifference:

"You have reported to the Ministry, I take it?"

"Yes, of course."

"And they are satisfied?"

"Oh, yes." His mind went back, without pleasure, to his talk with Milner the day before; the other man had been lugubrious as ever, and only convinced when he had himself perused the rambling pages of Lund's statement that—so far as General Aircraft were concerned, at least—the matter could be regarded as concluded. "There are still a lot of loose ends to tidy up," he added, "but they needn't concern you . . . or me."

"And the project?" Knowles had none of his colleague's stolidity, and eyed the visitor with his bird-like look of expectancy.

"Safe enough, it's up to your chaps now. From what Lund tells us, only one item of information was actually passed over; that was some time ago, a kind of earnest, I think, of what could be expected." He paused, and was uneasily conscious of Sir Thomas's air of intentness, of Knowles's troubled look. "Not that one can rely much on what he says now," he added. "But the whole thing was there, I'm told, on microfilm. In his brief case, I mean. And his idea seems to have been to go over to the other side in a blaze of glory."

"And all the trumpets sounded for him on the other side," said Knowles reflectively; and seemed to realise as he spoke the inapt nature of the quotation, so that his words trailed off in incoherent apology.

But neither of the others was giving him their attention. Antony had turned his chair, so that he could look down at the fire. He said abruptly: "He's raving now. There'll be no trial."

"Thank God for that!" said Knowles, with fervour.

"Yes, indeed." He moved restlessly, but went on after a moment. "The doctors are talking about a brain tumour, say he may not live long. That's something to be grateful for, too, I suppose?"

"I think so. The boy——"

"Poor Johnny. He was with us, you know, till Akeroyd took him with him to London last night. George would have taken him, I thought he'd hate the sight of us . . . because we were there; but he seemed to cling to Jenny."

"I am sure," said Sir Thomas, unsmiling, "that we are all very grateful to Mrs. Maitland——"

"You needn't be!" Maitland snapped. Knowles, seeing the danger signals, said hastily:

"There's an uncle in London. Mother's brother, sounds all right, I talked to him. The firm are going to look after the boy financially, take care of his education, whatever is necessary."

"That's a comfort." He divided a smile between the two men, but added as an afterthought: "You'll have to find him a new school; and don't be too sure you'll get a scientist out of it."

Knowles protested, a trifle incoherently. Sir Thomas, who seemed to find something amusing about the conversation, leaned forward with his elbows on the desk, and asked:

"That leads us—doesn't it?—to the questions we want answering. You were going to tell us——"

"Oh . . . well! What happened is easily told. I expect Lund was always dedicated to his work, and we'll never know at what point it reached the stage of a . . . a mania with him. Perhaps not until the 'Grass Snake' project was cancelled; though as his wife died only a year later, I should say that his preoccupation with his own job and Johnny's future must have started long before. I mean, it couldn't have been an easy decision."

"There's no doubt he killed his wife?"

"I'm afraid not. I hoped at first, for the boy's sake, that it was an illusion on his part, but his story—on that point—is circumstantial enough. He says it was easy . . . a window left open . . . a dose of medicine omitted; well, I suppose she might have died anyway, but the intention was there, and the effect on his mind was just as great. After that, the stage was set: he intended to collect full details of 'Full Moon' and make off with them; Johnny's education could then have continued in a less decadent atmosphere, I suppose, and he wouldn't have been distracted by outside claims to his interest. With this in view, he opened negotiations; and he seems to have been genuinely put out by the fact that an organisation immediately started to grow up about him. Appleby was imposed on him from outside, though he found his help invaluable; but the chap in Harrogate kept pressing for results, or at least something concrete to show for their labours . . . that seems to have infuriated Lund, but he produced a tidbit for them from time to time, and everyone was happy."

"I have wondered," said Knowles, "how you came to be present when Dick was killed."

"In a job like this it is elementary, of course, to look twice at anyone who shows signs of undue affluence. Appleby was hard up when he came to General Aircraft, now he seemed to have more money than he knew what to do with." He paused, and seemed to be considering this statement. "Well, to be accurate, it isn't quite as easy as that; I was suspicious of Basil for a time—and for quite the opposite reason."

"Oh, Basil!" said Knowles. "He's got a private venture of his own; some idea he means to take time to work on, when he's saved enough. If ever he does," he added, doubtfully, and seemed for a moment to be about to slip away from the discussion into a mournful contemplation of the cost of living.

"To get back to Appleby, then," said Antony firmly, "it seemed most likely that two people were concerned in Homer's death, so I cast him (tentatively, at that stage) for the role of accomplice. Later, it emerged that he had some cause of resentment—real or fancied—against Akeroyd. When I decided to make some attempt to bring him into the open, he made no admission but his remarks were illuminating. 'Why worry, they know it all,' he said. But that was later.

"Bill Homer died because he became suspicious, and his death was the only one of the three which could not, perhaps, have been avoided. Lund had been using him as a source of information, there was no reason at all why Homer should not speak freely to him, and even when his doubts were raised I think it would probably have been some time before he brought himself to do anything about them. But note the manner of his death; he stayed late at work on a night that turned out foggy . . . and if it hadn't been for what had been happening in the laboratory, nobody would ever have suspected that murder had been done.

"But Carleton's murder was another thing altogether.

Whoever he had seen on the night of the fog (and I think he deliberately deceived you, sir, when he spoke to you about it), whoever he had seen was most likely the decoy. I was guessing, frankly, in thinking it might have been Appleby. But there was no question that Carleton had been murdered; and no evidence either of the improvisation, the seizing of opportunity, that had characterised Homer's death. The way he died suggested a matter of impulse, and this was borne out by the fact that no attempt was made to move or hide his body. In the winter, as you know, Appleby generally came to work with Stephen Naylor; and didn't have too much difficulty getting a lift back to town if they happened to leave at different times in the evening. If, as I believe, he killed Carleton in a panic, because he was hinting at knowledge, he had probably no other choice than to drive away in the dead man's car, or walk into Mardingley and most likely be seen on the road.''

"So you think Dick killed Harry Carleton." Knowles was shaking his head over the thought. "I didn't realise——"

"Lund confirmed my suspicions on that point, and also says he helped dispose of the car later that night. It went into a bog on Egton moor, and they came back, comfortably, in Lund's Land-Rover. Lund was furious with Dick . . . he could see the foolishness of killing when somebody else was concerned; but he didn't hesitate when the same position arose with Richard Weston. Even so, I imagine he had more justification (if I can use that word in this context); Weston wouldn't be hinting, he would be *telling* him what he knew—probably that he had seen Appleby and Carleton together the night the latter disappeared. Lund didn't trust Dick . . . either his nerve or his common sense.

"Here again, we have the seized opportunity, the death that could have been taken for accident. But he wasn't so clever when it came to providing himself with an alibi; and this was the only real clue I had . . . the fact that he lied in saying he was taking Johnny to the pantomime on Boxing Day. He sent his housekeeper in his place, and told them both about the conversation at the party, and how he had made an excuse not to go shooting with Weston. 'So don't tell anybody I didn't go to Leeds,' he said, 'I wouldn't like to hurt his feelings.' ''

"That sounds quite reasonable to me," said Knowles.

"Yes, but when Weston was dead he could no longer make that a reason for their silence. Johnny thought 'a promise is a promise,' and didn't say anything; but Mrs. Whatever-her-name-is talked quite happily to Mrs. Ambler when Jenny put her up to cornering her in the Meadow Dairy last Friday. But that never occurred to Lund."

"A supreme egotist," said Sir Thomas, reflectively. And wondered why Maitland grinned at him.

"So one thing led to another," Knowles remarked. "Why did he kill Appleby?"

"Because he didn't trust him, and when I started showing my suspicions of Dick pretty clearly . . . well, I suppose it was my fault, but I can't say I shall lose much sleep over it. My idea was, that Lund would have a go at Stephen, probably trying to make it look like suicide."

"Appleby's death doesn't exactly fit in with your 'improvisation' theme," said Sir Thomas, a little smugly.

"I think it does. He certainly took the chance that offered, and what ought to have happened, you see, was that Dick just disappeared. If his body remained in the house, and no one knew he'd gone there, it might have been weeks before he was found, and Lund hoped to be away before then."

"There's one thing that isn't clear to me," said Knowles, "at what point did you begin to suspect that John was the man you were looking for?"

"You're asking me to account logically for a process of thought that was very far from that." He seemed to find the reflection a sad one, and sighed as he spoke. "I felt, early on, that he suspected my activities; perhaps that wasn't so surprising, but his habit of asking awkward questions didn't seem altogether in character. Both Stephen and George came in for my attention: in spite of his protests, Josiah obviously had his doubts about one or other of them, or why did he insist on a deputation of two when they came to see me? Evan Williams's preoccupation with security might well have been a blind; both he and Tom Burns kept cropping up, and both behaved, in varying degrees, abnormally. Tom's attitude, I felt, reflected not only suspicion of Stephen, but also some knowledge of Bill Homer's worries before he died; unfortunately, that wasn't helpful. As for Basil . . . he's a clever man, I couldn't help feeling if there were anything suspicious about him, he'd never let me see it; he seemed willing to be helpful, but I couldn't take that on trust. But until Weston was killed, my money was on him."

"But you haven't told us——"

"Oh, lord, I don't know . . . really. There were so many things: my own estimate of his character . . . what Basil told me (I found his remarks illuminating). . . . Akeroyd said 'John has blind spots for all his reliability.' Then, there was the boy; a perfectly ordinary lad, who was being forced into a mould he didn't fit. All quite normal, it happens every day. But enough to make me check up on the alibi; and *that* wasn't proof of anything."

"A guess," said Sir Thomas.

Maitland got up. "I'll admit that," he said. He sounded tired. "This kind of job, there rarely is legal proof; which makes it distressing, if you have a tidy mind. And it's one of the biggest risks you run . . . the chance of making a fool of yourself. This time, I happened to be right. It could just as easily have been the other way." He gestured towards the envelope, still on Sir Thomas's desk. "You won't find that any more illuminating," he said apologetically.

He was following Knowles out of the room a few moments later, when Sir Thomas called him back. "This report," he said, as Antony approached the desk again.

"For your directors," said Antony. "A matter of courtesy," he elaborated. "As you know, my responsibility was to the Ministry."

"Then it contains no mention——?" He seemed to find the sentence hard to complete, and Maitland took it up for him.

"Of Weston's activities? No."

"But . . . the Ministry——?"

"As I was satisfied the matter was irrelevant, there was no necessity to bring it up."

Sir Thomas was eyeing him closely. "I don't see how you could be satisfied," he said, in his forthright way. "I'm grateful, of course," he added.

"I asked my clerk to make some inquiries . . . he's a persistent sort of chap," Maitland explained. "He found someone who remembered a case you were involved in, years ago. You'd been called as a witness, but got out of it with a medical certificate; as the prosecution had a strong case they didn't ask for a postponement. The defendant was convicted, some sort of fraud. A well-known confidence trickster, my informant said. What did he sell you, a gold brick?"

He paused invitingly. Sir Thomas's mouth was shut like a trap, and his expression did not lighten. "I don't quite know what you're suggesting," he said at last.

"In words of one syllable, that your pride wouldn't allow you to have it published that once you were badly taken in. A stupid enough motive for submitting to blackmail: but perhaps you wouldn't have been such an easy victim if your own pocket had been touched. It's so easy in your position, and all you are doing is dispense a little patronage."

The older man pushed his chair back, and got up slowly. "I suppose in the circumstances I must overlook your insinuations," he said. "There will be, fortunately, no need for us to meet again."

"You can't even sack me!" said Antony sympathetically. He was smiling to himself as he turned away, but his expression was solemn enough when he turned in the doorway. "I shouldn't take it too much to heart," he advised. "They say he'd have fooled an archangel!" He was gone before Sir Thomas's exasperation could find further relief in words.

Mickey was making coffee, and the office—oddly—had taken on an air of festivity. The door to William Knowles's room was open, and after a few minutes he came through to join the gathering, as though unable to keep away from the talk that was going on. Evan Williams followed him; he seemed to be protesting about something, and Basil, catching Antony's eye, said with a grin: "We're getting back to normal, you see."

Stephen was sitting on a corner of Susie's desk. His colour was a little heightened this morning, and Antony guessed that his return among his colleagues for the first time since his release had been more of an ordeal than he would have cared to admit. Knowles beamed at him, but tactfully refrained from comment. Instead, he waved a hand towards Basil Vlasov and said to Antony: "Meet our new Chief of Research."

That was cause for rejoicing, certainly . . . perhaps they had seized on it as an excuse for relieving the tension they had all been under. Only Basil, when Antony made his way to his side a moment later, looked up at him sadly and murmured: "The king is dead——" He glanced round, and seeing that they were for the moment in a sort of isolation, he added: "You'll be seeing Johnny, won't you, in London?"

"We promised," said Maitland.

"Don't let him hate his father." The words came abruptly; and a moment later Basil, as though ashamed of a lapse into sentiment, added lamely: "It would be a pity——"

"Johnny'll be all right," he spoke confidently, and the other man retorted in a caustic tone:

"Don't tell me he'll rationalise the whole business."

"He'll learn to live with it, at least."

"Yes of course." He gave his companion one of his sidelong looks. "I like young Johnny."

"Then don't avoid him, don't try to be tactful. His parents' friends——"

Mickey interrupted them then, but Basil, who had been frowning over his thoughts, gave Antony a nod before the conversation became general. He stayed for half an hour, and was sorry when he felt it was time to go. The party from the lab went out ahead of him; Knowles had spoken of future meetings and departed for his own room; Mickey, with one of her wicked looks, lifted her face in obvious expectation of a farewell kiss; Susie embarrassed him hor-

ribly by saying, "Thank you, thank you," and bursting
into tears ("as though I'd done anything for that wretched
young man of hers," he told Jenny later, "beyond getting
him locked up—quite unnecessarily—for three days"). It
was left to Mickey to save the situation, saying roundly:
"He'd rather be kissed than cried at . . . any man would."
At which piece of feminine wisdom Susie dried her eyes
again.

Basil and Stephen were waiting below, beside the firm's
car that was to take him back to Mardingley. It was
another clear day, and the noise from the works was loud
and insistent. Everything was busy and orderly . . . the
stone had been cast, the ripples had spread and vanished
again, now there was nothing to show that there had ever
been a disturbance in the normal routine. Away to the
right, he could see the gate-house which guarded the
entrance to the Missile Division. Stephen followed his
glance. "You may not think so now, but it was worth
saving," he said in his abrupt way. Antony caught Basil's
eye, and laughed with real amusement.

"If you're going to get wrapped up in technicalities
again, it's time I was gone," he said. But examining his
feelings as he drove away, he was surprised to find regret
among them. By to-morrow his own life would have claimed
him again; but just at that moment he was an insignificant
member of the "Full Moon" team, and he was leaving
some good comrades behind him.

Back at Holly Royd, Jenny had just finished stowing the
suitcases in the back of the Jaguar. The bedroom looked
bleak now that their belongings were gone. Antony, root-
ing with a casual air through the empty chest of drawers,
asked suddenly:

"Are you sorry you stayed?"

"You know I'm not."

"It wasn't very pleasant, what I involved you in." The
bottom drawer revealed nothing to his suspicious look, and
he pushed it to with a decisive air and turned to face her.
"I didn't mean it to be like that," he said.

Jenny came up close to him. "You said 'we'll see it

through together'," she reminded him. "That's the way I wanted it." His look was sceptical. "Truly," she insisted.

Mrs. Ambler was in the hall when they came down a few moments later. Characteristically, she wasted no time in hustling them out to the car, but once there she detained Antony for a moment. "It's over now . . . isn't it?" she asked.

"Over and done with," he assured her. She looked past him then at Jenny, already in the driving seat. "That Stephen Naylor is talking about a wedding," she said. "If so be he's got his eye on Miss Susie, she's a good sort of lass. I'll be thinking if I can make a flat for them . . . I don't seem to have the heart to look for someone new."

"That's a splendid idea," said Jenny, with enthusiasm. "But I didn't know——"

"I don't think Susie knows either," said Antony as they drove away. An idea occurred to him, and he eyed her with sudden suspicion. "By the way, I've never asked you: that evening I asked Stephen to keep you company——"

Jenny gave him a look that was radiantly innocent. "What about it?" she said.